DATE DUE

DEC 27 1999	OCT 14 2001		
MAR 25 2000	MAR 01 2003		
NOV 25 2001	APR 28 2005		
FEB 24 2002	APR 16 2007		
NOV 12 2002	SEP 28 2011		
DEC 31 2003	FEB 06 2013		
JUL 19 2004			
MAY 22 2006	MAR 07 2014		
JUN 05 2006	AUG 24 2015		
OCT 20 2015			

ANIMORPHS®

The Decision

K.A. Applegate

AN
APPLE
PAPERBACK

SCHOLASTIC INC.
New York Toronto London Auckland Sydney

For Michael and Jake

Cover illustration by David B. Mattingly

ISBN 0-590-49441-4

12 11 10 9 8 7 9/9 0 1 2 3/0

Printed in the U.S.A. 40

First Scholastic printing, May 1998

CHAPTER 1

My name is Aximili-Esgarrouth-Isthill.

I don't know if my fellow Andalites will ever recognize that name. I guess some of the story I'm about to tell will appear in the scientific journals. I mean, the accident that occurred to me has certainly rewritten the science of Zero-space mass extrusion during morphing.

But I doubt that my real name will be used. I doubt that the whole truth will be told. And I guess that's a good thing. You see, there are traitors among us. Yes, traitors among our fellow Andalites. Andalites working for the Yeerks.

I am the only living Andalite witness to the *Ascalin* incident. Only I — and my human friends, Prince Jake, Cassie, Tobias, Rachel, and

Marco — know what truly happened aboard that ship on war-torn planet Leera. And even though I know what happened, I will never know *why* it happened.

I know it seems impossible even to conceive of Andalites as traitors. I know the very idea makes any decent Andalite sick inside. But I am telling the truth. The *Ascalin* incident happened. We were betrayed by one of our own.

My name is Aximili-Esgarrouth-Isthill, brother of Elfangor-Sirinial-Shamtul. And I swear by his memory that everything I say here is true.

I am the only Andalite presently located on planet Earth. Don't bother looking Earth up on any of the databases. You won't find much information. The truth is, we lost a Dome ship in orbit above this planet. The Yeerks destroyed it. We lost my brother, Prince Elfangor, in that battle, too. But before he died, Elfangor broke our law and gave the secret Andalite morphing power to five human youths.

The Yeerks are after this planet now. They are invading Earth in their usual style. The Yeerk parasite slugs have an easy time entering human heads, wrapping themselves around human brains. Enslaving humans as they did the Hork-Bajir and the Gedds. As they hope someday to do to us.

I live among these humans now. With the group of young humans who were given the morphing power by Elfangor. They call themselves Animorphs. They resist the Yeerk invasion of Earth. All alone, as far as we know.

I live with humans. I respect them. But my hearts are still Andalite. No matter what anyone ever says about me and about what happened on Leera, I am true to my own people.

And yet there are times when I wonder: Who are my *own* people? My race, my species? My family? My friends? My allies?

My human friends insist on reducing my name to "Ax." You see, humans communicate by making mouth-sounds. (Most Andalites understand the concept of a "mouth," I believe.) And although my full name is easily pronounced in Andalite thought-speak, it is somewhat long and complex for primitive human mouth-sounds.

I am alone on this planet. The only one of my species. The only Andalite among all the humans. So I have used the morphing technology to create a human morph. And sometimes, for two hours at a time, I become human and pass among humans as one of them.

I am very good at passing for human, if I say so myself. I have learned the customs and habits perfectly so that I seem entirely normal.

That's how I am able to pass even in the most human of places. For example, the mall. Which is a place full of shops, most of which sell artifi-

cial skin and artificial hooves. Technically known as "clothing" and "shoes."

The mall also houses the most wonderful eating places. You see, in addition to making sounds with their mouths, humans use them to eat. They place foods into the mouth opening and grind the foods with teeth while adding saliva. This involves a sense called "taste."

Taste is very, very powerful.

Oh, yes.

I was wearing artificial skin and artificial hooves like a human. I approached the counter of my very favorite eating place.

"Hello," I said, making mouth-sounds with my human mouth. "I will work for money. Muh-nee. Mnee."

I should explain: Money is a sort of abstract human concept. You give amounts of money to various people in society and they in turn give you useful items.

"Do you want to order something?" the human said to me.

"I require money so that I may exchange it for the delicious cinnamon buns," I explained.

The human blinked his eyes. "So . . . you *do* want to order, or you *don't*?"

Obviously this was a less-intelligent human. "I wish to perform labor, lay-ber, lay-burrr, and to have you give me money. Then I wish to use that money to acquire delicious cinnamon buns. Bun-zuh."

"I'll get the manager."

"Bun-zuh," I said. I find the "z" sound especially enjoyable. It tickles the mouthparts. Many sounds are amusing.

The manager came and I explained my request to her.

"Well, I can't give you a job," she said. "I think you're under age. But I guess if you're hungry I could have you clear some of those tables and give you some food."

This was acceptable to me.

"Poor kid," she said to the other human as I turned away. "A little off in the head, maybe. But a good-looking boy."

I soon discovered what she meant by clearing tables. In this part of the mall there are many tables, surrounded by eating places. The tables were littered with delicious things!

On the first table I found thin, crisp, salty-greasy triangles covered with a bright yellow secretion. I ate them and they were very good.

On the next table were liquids. I drank them. One was hot, one was cold. Along with the liquids was a square of crumpled paper. Smeared inside the paper was a reddish, semiliquid product. I licked it. It was fine, but not wonderful.

Then at last, I saw what I wanted. Two large,

steaming hot, glistening cinnamon buns. Two humans were sitting very near the cinnamon buns.

They were going to eat my buns!

I raced over as quickly as my wobbly human legs could go. "I am clearing these tables!" I cried.

The humans looked at me. "We haven't even eaten yet."

"Good," I said, relieved. I grabbed the two cinnamon buns and carried them away.

"Hey! Hey, stop!"

I began to shove the first bun into my mouth. Oh, the joy! Oh, how can I even explain to an Andalite who has never possessed the sense of taste? The sensation! It was a pleasure beyond any pleasure imaginable. The warmth, the dripping, sweet goo of the cinnamon bun!

"What are you doing?" the manager cried as she came running over.

"I amm glearing khe khables," I said. It is very difficult to speak while eating. Just one of the many design flaws in humans.

"I am terribly sorry," the manager said to the humans who were trying to take my cinnamon buns. "I'll get you two fresh buns. And *you*," she said, pointing one of her powerful-yet-stubby human fingers at me, "come with me."

She pulled me away, causing me to drop a small portion of the bun from my mouth. She took me into the eating place and made me sit on a chair. This involves bending the two legs and resting the weight of the body on a raised platform by pressing the fatty pads at the top of the legs against the platform. It's hard to visualize unless you've seen it.

"Okay, now look, son, if you're that desperate for food, there's a tray of buns here that are just a bit stale. You can help yourself. You poor kid."

She indicated a square array of cinnamon buns. Perhaps a dozen in all!

"For me?" I asked in a voice choked with emotion.

"Sure, son. Go ahead and have one."

Let me make one final point here: human mouth-sound language is very fuzzy at times. "Have one," she'd said.

One mouthful? One bun?

One tray?

It was certainly not my fault if there was any confusion.

CHAPTER 2

"So, there I am," Marco said. "Cruising through the food court, minding my own business, thinking, *Hey, why not snag a taco?* when I notice the paramedics and this crowd all gathered around the Cinnabon."

Marco is one of my human friends. He is shorter than some humans of his age. He has dark hair and dark eyes and likes to make jokes. Jokes are humor. Humor is more common among humans than among Andalites.

I think they have to resort to humor. It helps them deal with the embarrassment of being so wobbly on their two ridiculous legs.

"And I swear, it was like this sudden, psychic feeling. I knew, I mean, I *knew* somehow the Ax-man was involved. So I go over and ask someone in the crowd what's happening. And she says —"

"*She*?" Rachel interrupted. "Let me guess. Some good-looking girl who normally would never even talk to you? But you figured since there's a medical emergency that would be a good time to hit on her?"

"Exactly," Marco said.

Rachel is a female. She has gold hair and blue eyes. She is tall for her age.

"Anyway, she tells me, 'Some kid went crazy and ate an entire pan of cinnamon buns.' Now, who, I ask you all, *who* do we know who would eat an entire pan of cinnamon buns?"

Marco, Rachel, and the others — Prince Jake, Cassie, and Tobias — all looked at me and stretched their mouths horizontally to make grins. All except Tobias, who is a *nothlit*: a person trapped in morph. He is a hawk and has no lips.

I felt I had to say something. <I was not aware of the precise specifications for human stomachs,> I explained. <It seems there is some sort of limit on the quantity that may be consumed. Passing that limit caused an unpleasant sensation in the stomach area. It also caused me to become dizzy.>

"The sugar rush of all time," Cassie said.

Cassie is no taller than Marco. She has dark hair and eyes. Cassie is very interested in ani-

mals. By "animals," humans mean all animals aside from themselves.

I was out of my human morph and back in my own body. We were in the forest that begins at the edge of Cassie's farm. This is where I live. Tobias and me both. He eats mice, mostly in the morning. I leave the forest at night and go running across the fields, absorbing grass through my hooves, the way any sensible creature should.

We were waiting there in the woods for the arrival of a strange ally: Erek, the Chee.

The Chee are a race of androids. They were created by a now-dead race called Pemalites. The Chee and the last remaining Pemalites came to Earth thousands of years ago. They were escaping the devastation of their home world. The Pemalites did not survive. Their principled, nonviolent, but shockingly powerful androids did.

Prince Jake looked at his watch. Humans are always lost in time. They are constantly certain that "it" is later or earlier than they thought. I have never known a human to say, "Oh, look, it's exactly what time I thought it was."

Prince Jake said, "I was about to mention that Erek was late, but I guess it's still earlier than I thought it was."

You see what I mean.

<He's coming now,> Tobias said. <He can

move very quietly when he wants to. But I can see him from up here.>

Hawks have excellent hearing and really extraordinary powers of sight. But still, they can only look in one direction at a time, just like humans.

Erek approached — exactly on time, of course. He appears to be a normal human boy. But of course that is merely a very advanced holographic illusion. Beneath the hologram is an android of gray and white metals, somewhat resembling an Earth dog walking on two legs.

The Chee are incapable of violence. A prohibition against violence is written into their programming. Yet with our help, Erek was once able to disable that programming. He saved our lives in a terrible battle. But he chose then to surrender the power to do violence.

However, even though they cannot do battle, the Chee have managed to infiltrate the Yeerk organization on Earth. And from time to time Erek brings us useful information.

"Hi everyone," Erek said.

"Hey, Erek," Marco said. "What's up?"

Erek shrugged, exactly like any other young human of his apparent age. "Not much. Just something strange. Something that doesn't make sense. At least not as far as we can see."

Prince Jake nodded. He looked up at Tobias. "Are we clear?"

Tobias dropped from the branch he was on, flapped his wings, and soared above the treetops out of sight.

"Sorry," Prince Jake said to Erek. "I want to be sure we're safe."

Erek made an amused grin. "Do you think I came alone? Three of my people are spread out around us, keeping watch. Tobias will never spot them, not even with his eyes."

"Oh? Want to put some money on that?" Prince Jake asked.

Tobias flew back and landed on the same branch. He began to calmly preen his feathers. <All clear.>

"You didn't see anything at all?" Prince Jake asked, sounding disappointed.

<Well, I saw two Chee projecting tree holograms, and another one trying to pass himself off as a rock, but nothing to worry about.>

The humans and Erek all laughed.

<I *know* these woods,> Tobias said smugly. <You think you can just park some big old holographic willow tree where it doesn't belong and I won't notice? Puh-leeze.>

Erek did a sort of bow toward Tobias. "Remind me never to underestimate you, brother hawk." Then, suddenly serious, he told us what he'd come to say.

"The second-ranking guy in the Secret Service, a man named Hewlett Aldershot the Third, is in a hospital in a coma. He was hit by a car while walking across the street. We don't know why he's here in this area. But we do know this: No one even knows he's in the hospital."

"His family doesn't know?" Cassie said.

"No. No one. Not his family, not his boss, Jane Carnegie. No one. The hospital is heavily infiltrated by Yeerks. Half the staff are human-Controllers. His name isn't even in the hospital computers. And, oh, by the way, the car that hit him? A minivan belonging to none other than our friend Chapman."

Prince Jake nodded. He is the leader of the Animorphs. I consider him to be my prince. As an *aristh*, I require someone to be my prince.

"Well, well," Prince Jake said. "I guess we'd better check it out."

CHAPTER 3

<I have a question,> Marco said. <If you already have a Hewlett Aldershot and a Hewlett Aldershot, Jr., what kind of parent is going to go and inflict that name on a third kid? He must have gotten beat up after school every single day of his life.>

It was the next day. Marco, Rachel, and I were on the ledge of a third-story window. We were in seagull morph. According to my human friends, seagulls are like pigeons. They can go anywhere without looking suspicious.

I am sure they are right. Although I have no idea what a pigeon is. Nor can I imagine what a "suspicious" bird might be.

<I'm just saying for all we know, Chapman

just ran this guy down because he couldn't stand that name.>

Rachel sighed. <Why does Jake make me go on missions with you, Marco?>

<What, I shouldn't talk? I shouldn't make conversation? We've been hanging around on this stupid ledge for an hour and a half. Me, you, and Ax.>

<Just an hour and a half?> Rachel said. <Funny, it seems so much longer. The time when you're talking just drags on and on and on, Marco. On and on and on and —>

<Very funny.>

<Actually, it has only been one of your hours and eighteen minutes,> I said helpfully.

<One of *our* hours,> Marco said. <You know, they really are *your* hours now, too. This is Earth. You're stuck here. Go ahead and set your watch to local time.>

Marco was bored. We all were. But Marco gets snappish when he's bored.

We were on the sill outside the private hospital room of Hewlett Aldershot the Third. This was our second shift on the windowsill. We'd done a shift earlier in the morning, waiting for close to the two-hour limit. Then Prince Jake and Cassie had taken a turn, then it was back to us.

<This is so totally not what I want to be doing on a beautiful Saturday with major sales on at

Express *and* Old Navy,> Rachel complained. <It's my turn to go fly around. Be right back.>

She flapped away, leaving me and Marco. We fluttered our wings a little and jerked our heads and marched back and forth on the stone sill. We were trying to act like seagulls. That's why Rachel had to fly off. It was the right thing for a seagull to do.

<Is there something unusual about the name Hewlett Alder — look!> I said, interrupting myself. <A new human is entering the room. And I believe he is familiar.>

<Rachel!> Marco yelled in thought-speak. <Go find Jake and Cassie and Tobias. We have company!>

<Who?>

<Visser Three in his human morph,> I said. <The Abomination!>

Seagulls have eyes on the sides of their heads. So I turned one eye to stare in through the window. Yes, it was him. Visser Three, leader of the invasion of Earth.

Visser Three is, of course, the only Yeerk ever to successfully seize and infest an Andalite body. When he took that body, he also got the Andalite morphing power that went with it. So only Visser Three, among all the Yeerks in the universe, has the power to morph.

I felt the slow rage I always feel on seeing the

foul creature, my brother's murderer. Once I came close to avenging my brother. Once I almost destroyed Visser Three. But in the end, I failed, and he still lives.

The next time there will be no mistakes.

<Whoa. Visser Three, and in human morph,> Marco said nervously. <Definitely something major going on.>

Two human doctors came into the room. They spoke to the Visser. They spoke respectfully. Fearfully. Shaking. I could not hear them through the glass, but clearly they knew who and what Visser Three was.

Visser Three began to demorph. To return to Andalite form. From the human head, the twin stalk eyes appeared. From the human chest, the front two legs began to grow. From the base of the human spine, the long, swift, dangerous Andalite tail began to extend.

To my left, a swift flash of brown and tan with a hint of red. Tobias, swooping past. I kept my other eye focused through the glass.

The blue and tan fur rippled across the formerly human skin. Visser Three was on four legs now, tail cocked and ready.

<He is very sure he's safe in this place,> I said. <Otherwise he would never demorph like this.>

<The doctors aren't too happy, though,> Marco observed.

The doctors were shaking. Obviously, something was wrong. Then in a flash, Visser Three pressed his tail blade against one doctor's throat.

One twitch would send the doctor's head rolling across the floor.

Now that he was back in his Andalite body, we could hear Visser Three's unguarded thought-speak. <I gave orders that this human be cured!> he raged. <There is no point placing one of our people in his head if he's unable to move.>

The doctor said something. Something very respectful, very careful.

<I don't care about his brain stem, I want him repaired! Do you have any idea how useful this human would be to us? He is the number two man in the organization that guards their president. He would have access to half the secrets on this planet. That's why I arranged for him to be injured and brought here.>

Prince Jake and Cassie flew by, both in seagull morph.

<What's up?> Prince Jake asked.

<Visser Three, Prince Jake.>

<Don't call me "prince." Yeah, I hear his thought-speak. I meant, what do you see?>

<The Visser is busy terrorizing a pair of human-Controller doctors,> I said.

Just then, Visser Three withdrew his tail blade. The doctor collapsed and fell to his knees on the floor. His fellow doctor looked at him with pity, but made no move to help him.

<You leave me with no choice: If I can't use this creature as a host, I'll have to acquire him and morph him. I can't spend all my time in his form. I can't live his life. But using him, I can get close to his superior. I can use this morph to seize her instead!>

The doctor who was still standing spoke. He smiled. He looked encouraging and enthusiastic. The Visser flicked his tail, hit the doctor with the flat of the blade, and knocked him across the room.

<Don't tell me "It's all worked out for the best,"> Visser Three sneered. <I still want this human repaired. That's the only reason I let you live. Three days from now this human will be well, or the two of you will be very, very . . . very . . . sick.>

Then one stalk eye turned to stare directly at me. The second stalk eye followed. And I began to have a very bad feeling.

CHAPTER 4

Visser Three moved away, out of sight.

<Was he eyeballing us?> Marco asked. Then he answered his own question. <He *was* eyeballing us.>

<Prince Jake,> I said in thought-speak only my friends could hear. <What should we do?>

<What's happened?> Prince Jake asked.

<He eyeballed us, that's what happened,> Marco said.

<The Visser has moved out of our sight,> I said.

<Okay. Look, he may suspect you're not real seagulls,> Prince Jake said. <So don't behave suspiciously, or like you notice him. One of you

fly off. The other one wait a few seconds, then fly off. Like normal —>

CRASH!

The glass window exploded outward as something came blasting out through it. Marco was knocked from the sill and went tumbling, out of control, toward the ground.

I was too shocked to react at first.

Then I saw what had come bursting through the window. A *kafit* bird! A six-winged *kafit* bird!

It had to be Visser Three in morph. But how?

<Impossible!> I cried in total shock. The *kafit* bird only lives in one place in the universe: the Andalite home world.

The *kafit* shook off the glass shards and banked sharply back toward me. Its razor-sharp, killing beak was aimed at me like a missile.

I dropped from the sill, wings folded. The deadly beak missed me by a feather! I opened my wings, caught air, and flapped hard.

The *kafit* was on me! The six wings gave it terrific speed.

<Ax, what is that thing?> Cassie cried.

I didn't have time to answer. My human friends didn't understand. The *kafit* lives by spearing tree-living creatures. It is fast, accurate, and deadly to small creatures.

And at the moment, I was a small creature.

<Everyone on that bird!> Prince Jake roared. <He can't take us all. Tobias! Where are you?>

<Too far away,> Tobias said grimly.

I turned my head to look for the *kafit*. Stupid! My head acted like a rudder and made me turn. Right into the path of the *kafit*!

I flapped wildly, crazily. Too slow! The *kafit*'s beak sliced through the underside of my wing.

<Aaaahhh!> I yelled.

I turned and flew in abject panic. I flapped my wings and skimmed twenty feet above the ground. I knew the *kafit* was faster. Was it more agile, too?

But part of my mind just kept asking, <How, how, how?>

How had Visser Three acquired the DNA of a *kafit* bird? Had the Abomination actually set foot on Andalite grass?

I was flying over a major street now. What the humans call fast-food restaurants were below me. The Visser was inches behind me. He'd have me in three . . . two. . . . I flared, killed my speed, twisted my tail and head to shoot me sideways, and the *kafit* bird blew past.

He was faster. I could out-turn him, but only when I had the benefit of surprise. How many more times could I trick him that way?

<A nice maneuver, Andalite,> the Visser said,

his thought-speak suddenly in my head. <Why not try it again?>

I was almost angry enough to answer. But of course Visser Three could not be sure I was an Andalite in morph. He was guessing. If I remained silent he might decide I was just an innocent seagull who happened to be on the sill.

I saw Prince Jake and the others racing to catch up.

<Prince Jake! Do not help me. If you help me he'll know for sure that we are not just birds.>

<Stop being a hero,> Prince Jake said. <Tobias!>

<I'm doing the best I can. I got dead air here!> Tobias yelled.

I caught a flash of the big red-tailed hawk laboring to get altitude for a killing dive. But he was no more than ten feet above me and too far off to the side to help.

I was on my own.

Fine. So much the better, I said to myself, trying to sound braver than I felt. I flapped madly toward a large golden sign in the shape of two conjoined arches. <Let's see just how fast the *kafit* bird can turn.>

I aimed straight for the hole in one arch, shot through it, and instantly turned. Visser Three rocketed past, outside the arch, and turned to

come back toward me. But now I reversed and went back through the second arch. The *kafit* was after me, but now his greater speed was useless. And his broad wingspan made it tough to fit through the arches.

Visser Three circled at blazing speed, but I threaded my way again and again through the arches.

<Good job, Ax-man!> Tobias cried. <Hang in there. I have him in my sights!>

Humans were gathering beneath us, gaping up at the bizarre spectacle.

"Hey, that bird has too many wings!" one yelled.

"Must be a mutant bird. Go seagull, go!"

Whap! My wing tip caught the edge of an arch. I stuttered through the air. I missed my turn.

<Aaaaahhhh!>

The razor-sharp beak cut an inch from my wing tip! I fell. I hit the black roof of the fast-food restaurant. I staggered and hopped into a narrow space between two large, loud cooling units.

I saw the Visser swoop by low overhead and I knew that he had landed on the roof, too.

I began to demorph as fast as I could. The roof was surrounded by a raised wall. The humans on the ground could not see us. And once I was Andalite again, the bird would pose no more threat.

From my talons, hooves began to grow. My tail feathers melted together and formed the beginnings of my tail blade. But as I grew, the space became tight. I was wedged in between the cooling units, with fans blasting me with greasy smells.

I forced my way out, half Andalite, half bird, staggering on misshapen legs. Out into the open center of the roof. And there I saw him. Like me, he was demorphing. Like me, he was part bird, part Andalite.

But this was no true Andalite.

<Give yourself up, Andalite,> the Visser sneered. <And I may even let you live.>

<Let's see how good you are tail to tail,> I said, once more trying to sound far more confident than I was.

His tail emerged. My tail emerged.

And we stood, seemingly two Andalites, preparing for a battle to the death.

I looked into the eyes of the Abomination. And there I saw evil.

And then I saw something that made my hearts leap. Because I also saw fear.

CHAPTER 5

It had been a very long time since any Andalites fought tail to tail, except as part of military training or as a sport.

And this was no sport.

There, amid the blowing fans and the smell of grease and fried meat, Visser Three and I stood face-to-face.

Two seagulls fluttered down to land. Then two more. My stalk eye noted the predator's outline of a hawk on the wing overhead.

<Let's demorph,> Rachel said, directing her thought-speak to include me. I hoped she'd remember not to let Visser Three hear it. Humans sometimes forget that thought-speak can be targeted to everyone or just a list of people.

<We can't demorph,> Prince Jake said to me. <We'd have to pass through our human forms first. We can't demorph unless we are absolutely sure Visser Three is not going to walk away from this.>

<If we demorph, he *won't* walk away,> Rachel said grimly.

I kept my eyes trained on the Visser. My tail was on a hair trigger. The slightest movement and I would strike.

I said, <Prince Jake, we can't take the chance. If he ever learns you are humans, your lives will be worthless. I can avenge Elfangor alone.>

<This isn't the place,> Cassie said reasonably. <People down below saw a six-winged bird come up here. Someone is probably on their way.>

I barely heard her. The Visser was edging sideways, looking for an opening. I arched my tail blade high, ready to block his attack.

<Ax, can you back off without getting hurt?> Prince Jake asked. <Cassie's right. We don't want this fight here.>

Part of me wanted to say, yes, yes, we can let the Visser escape. He was bigger than I. His tail would have a half-foot advantage in reach. He was taller, which made it easier for him to strike my eyes, my head.

But another part of me had seen that look of fear in the Visser's eyes. He'd realized he was in a trap. He'd realized he was facing a battle to the death where the odds were not all that favorable to him.

I wanted to see more of that fear from him. I wanted to see the terror as I pressed my tail blade against his throat and said, <This is for my brother.>

Sudden movement!

I struck! My tail blade missed its target, but slashed the Abomination across his shoulder.

In the confusion, I didn't understand at first. Everything happened at once: his sudden movement, my strike, and then, the graceful flight as his leap took him over the wall.

He fell from sight. I ran to the edge and craned to look over.

A human girl below was crying, "I swear I saw a blue horse jump off the roof!"

"You're crazy. Where'd it land, then?" her friend said.

I could see where he'd landed. In a large square trash bin.

"In that Dumpster," the first girl said.

I glared down at the Visser. His left rear leg was broken from the fall. He was morphing to human as fast as he could. He looked up at me with eyes blazing hatred.

I wanted to say something. I wanted to shout some threat. Make some dire promise. But all I did was stare eye to eye with Visser Three.

And then, as his human mouth appeared, he sneered.

<Come on, Ax,> Prince Jake said. <We're done here.>

CHAPTER 6

That night I ran across the far pastures of Cassie's ranch and tried to figure out my emotions.

It was a wet night. Rain was falling, although not hard by Earth standards. The grass was wet and moist. I could feel my hooves picking up the worms that come out of the ground when it's wet. There would be extra protein in my diet, which was the last thing I needed. Too much protein keeps me awake.

The clouds overhead hid the moon and the stars. This made me sad. I like to find the home star at night. It has become a sort of unofficial ritual. Something I do for myself. To remind myself that there is a place for me in the galaxy. I may not be there, but the place does exist.

Or am I just fooling myself? Yes, I have a home planet. And a home on that planet. And a people like me. But will I ever fit in there again? Have I changed too much, been with humans too long?

I saw the lights of Cassie's home. Once I had morphed into Prince Jake and gone there for dinner with Cassie's parents. I have Prince Jake's DNA from the time when he became infested by a Yeerk.

It's a treasured memory. Dinner with Cassie, I mean, not morphing Prince Jake. Sometimes when I'm alone in the woods and thinking about home, I find myself thinking about that evening instead.

I ran faster now, no longer concerned with eating, but just wanting to feel the impact of raindrops on my face and my chest. If I could run fast enough, all the drops would hit my face and chest and none would fall down on my back.

I saw a wooden rail fence. Almost too high to jump. But I ran straight at it, kicked, tucked my front legs, and sailed over.

There was a "thump!" as one hoof nicked the top rail.

I landed easily and realized I was panting. I slowed down and trotted back toward the woods.

I could have beaten him, I told myself. *I could have forced the fight. I could have struck again before he had a chance to get away.*

Another part of my mind answered, *No, you would have lost. He's taller, bigger. He's more experienced. The Andalite body Visser Three controls used to belong to a great warrior. Visser Three has all of that warrior's skill and experience.*

You went tail to tail with Visser Three and let him get away.

I went tail to tail with Visser Three and at least I didn't run away.

You wanted to. You were frightened.

I'd be a fool not to be frightened. But I didn't run. He did.

I realized I'd come to rest, standing beneath a particularly tall pine tree just back from the edge of a meadow. Tobias's meadow.

<What's up, Ax-man?> he called down from the darkness above.

<Are you awake?>

<Yeah. I have this slight tendency to wake up when big, blue, scorpion-tailed alien centaurs go crashing around in the woods like a herd of ruptured elephants.>

Tobias is sometimes harsh when awakened. It is a human characteristic that he has not lost.

<I apologize for waking you. How do elephants come to be ruptured?>

Tobias sighed. He floated down to a lower branch, then sailed over to a fallen log. <You're stewing, aren't you?>

<What?>

<Stewing. Going over things again and again in your head. Around and around in circles, asking yourself the same questions again and again, then starting it all over again.>

<How did you know?>

<Look, Ax, the first time I saw Visser Three . . . and you know when that was . . . I cried, I was so scared.>

<He was an alien. He was unfamiliar to you.>

<Elfangor was an alien. He was unfamiliar. He didn't scare me. Visser Three did. Not because of what he looked like, but because I could feel something coming from him. Like a dark cloud. Like a smell, almost. This *feeling*, I don't know any other word for it. Like I was looking at something that needed to be destroyed. He was evil. I felt it. And I had this horrible understanding, this knowledge, that one way or the other, that evil was going to touch me and change me. So I just cried.>

<I have met Visser Three before,> I said stonily. <I should not have been afraid.>

<What could you have done?>

<I could have forced the fight.>

<What if you'd lost?>

<What if I'd won? It would have been a terrible blow against the Yeerks. I would have avenged Elfangor. I would have done a great service for my people.>

<Look, Ax, you went up against him. He backed down. Not you.>

<He was surrounded and outnumbered. He thought each of you was another Andalite warrior ready to demorph and attack. He retreated with honor.>

<Honor,> Tobias said derisively. <He's a cold-blooded killer. He's an invader in someone else's land. He's just another gangster. Murderers don't have honor.>

<I should let you go back to sleep.>

<Ooookay. You want to drop it, it's dropped.> He looked around, blinking, almost as blind as a human in the darkness. <Hard to sleep when it's raining, anyway.>

<Tobias. The bird that Visser Three morphed? It was an Andalite bird. It's called a *kafit* bird. From my home planet.>

<You're thinking, what? That Visser Three

must have been on the Andalite home world in order to acquire it?>

<Yes. I am worried that the Abomination has set foot on the Andalite home world.>

I felt Tobias grow tense. Now he was beginning to understand. But he said, <Sometimes people must take animals off the home world, right? I mean, just the way you can find an African lion in a zoo in America, Europe, wherever. Right? So, okay, someone totally innocent takes one of these birds off your planet. They get hijacked or whatever. And it ends up in Visser Three's hands.>

I wanted to believe it was possible. So I said, <Yes, that could be it.>

But I didn't believe it. I believed that Visser Three had either been to my world. Or that some ally of his had been there.

Either way it meant only one thing. The Yeerks had begun to reach into the one safe place in the galaxy: my home.

CHAPTER 7

We met at the barn where Cassie and her father care for sick or injured nonhuman animals. It is called the Wildlife Rehabilitation Clinic. It is a large, dark building made of wood. Within it are numerous cages made of steel wire. And within the cages are the sick animals.

Tobias was high in the rafters. From up there he can see out through a sort of window and can warn us if anyone is approaching.

Everyone else was on the ground level. Cassie was working, pushing piles of dirty hay with a very large, three-pronged fork. Prince Jake would occasionally lift something out of her way.

Marco and Rachel were just chilling.

That's what humans call it. I believe it refers

to the fact that when humans sit very still and do nothing, their body temperature drops. Thus, "chilling."

Someday, when I am old, too old to be a warrior, I will write a book about humans and their strange habits and speech and technology. For example, did you know that humans invented books *before* computers? Because of this they believe computers to be superior, despite the very obvious fact that it takes one of their computers as much as thirty seconds to "load" a page, while a book page can be accessed with zero effective delay.

One would almost dismiss humans as a quaint, unimportant, backward race. Except for two things. First, these are, after all, the creatures who have raised the art of taste to incredible levels. Humans may be technologically primitive, but they have created buttered popcorn, the Snickers bar, chili, and cigarette butts. (Although humans themselves become very upset by the idea of eating cigarette butts.)

And let us not forget: Humans, for all their faults, have created the cinnamon bun. Someday, after the war, there will be pilgrimages of Andalites streaming to Earth to morph into humans for a day and do nothing but eat cinnamon buns.

Get the extra frosting. It's worth it.

"Ax, are you paying attention?" Marco asked.

I snapped out of my daydream. <Yes, of course.>

"Because, see, I've said the same thing to you twice now, and you just keep staring off into space like you're a million miles away."

<Please tell me a third time and I will pay attention.>

"I said, by Visser Three morphing an Andalite bird, maybe he was sending a message. I mean, he still thinks we're all Andalites. He was pretty sure he was chasing an Andalite in morph, right? So he chooses to morph an Andalite bird? That's not a coincidence. That's a message."

And that's the second reason not to dismiss humans as unimportant. They are unbelievably quick to adapt. Just a few months ago, Marco didn't believe there was life on other planets. Now he's accepted that fact, absorbed an entirely new world view, found himself in the middle of a war using morphing technology he doesn't understand, and even managed to have insights that I miss.

<Yes,> I said slowly. <Yes. But why? What message?>

Marco shrugged his shoulders. "He's rattling your cage. It's like, 'Hey, pal, while you're stuck here on Earth I've been in and out of your house, hanging out with your buddies, and eating your mom's cookies.'"

<My mother does not make cookies,> I pointed out. <The sense of taste is unknown among —>

"The Visser's yanking your chain," Rachel said.

"Messing with your mind," Cassie agreed.

<Jerking you around,> Tobias said.

"Trying to baffle you with . . . oh, never mind," Prince Jake said. "The point is, you have two questions: How did Visser Three acquire this bird? And why did he morph it to attack you?"

"That's not the real question, though," Cassie said. "The real question is what are we going to do about this Hewlett Aldershot the Third?"

Marco stuck up his hand. "Get him to change his name?"

"You know, it's a pretty good plan Visser Three has," Prince Jake pointed out. "He acquires our man Hewlett Aldershot the Third, then he walks into work at the Secret Service offices, punches up anything he wants on the computer, sits in on secret conferences, and ends up knowing everything the Secret Service knows."

<What does the Secret Service know?> I asked.

"A lot," Marco said.

<Ah.>

"It's not just what he can find out, it's who he can talk to and get access to," Rachel said. "He can find out if any information about Yeerk activities ever gets to —"

"Whoa!" Marco shot straight up on his two wobbly legs. I can never get past thinking humans will topple over when they do that.

"What whoa?" Prince Jake asked mildly.

"Whoa, as in whoa, Rachel is right. H.A. Third can talk to anyone, right? He can talk to his boss, right? So, if he was to walk in and say, 'Boss, guess what? Parasite slugs from outer space are invading Earth!' Well, okay, they'd throw him in the nuthouse. *But* if he was to walk in and say, 'Parasite slugs from outer space are invading Earth, and guess what, I can turn into a rhinoceros, and then he actually *did* turn into a rhinoceros . . . well. Suddenly, boom! The secret is out. The Yeerks are screwed."

"Unless his boss is a Controller," Rachel said.

"If she were a Controller, why would Visser Three be bothering with H.A. Third?" Cassie pointed out. But then she turned to Marco. "What exactly are you thinking? Are you talking about morphing Mr. Aldershot?"

"Duh. Yeah."

"We don't do that," Cassie said. "I thought we decided we don't do that. We don't morph humans."

<I morphed Prince Jake,> I said. I was excited by Marco's idea. But there are times when my human friends are reluctant to do whatever it takes to hurt the Yeerks. Sometimes so am I.

<And Cassie morphed Rachel that time,> Tobias said.

"First of all, Ax, you're not a human, so maybe it's okay if you morph Jake. Besides, Jake would have given his permission if he hadn't been infested with a Yeerk. And Rachel *did* give me her permission," Cassie said.

"Excuse me," Marco said with an edge of sarcasm in his voice. "Our man H.A. Third can't give permission. He's a vegetable. He's a carrot. He's a cabbage. He's a tomato."

"I thought tomatoes were fruit," Rachel interrupted, trying to provoke Marco.

"It's called a 'persistent vegetative state,' thanks so much for your sensitivity, Marco," Cassie said. "But we don't know if Mr. Aldershot is that bad off. He could just be in a coma. We don't have the right to go stealing his DNA."

"The man is a brussels sprout," Marco said.

"We'd never get in there, anyway," Prince Jake said. "Visser Three knows we know. We have to be in human form to 'acquire' Aldershot's DNA. You think we could do that with Visser Three on guard? Not likely."

Everyone looked downcast. Prince Jake was correct.

But then Cassie said, "Oh, man."

"What?" Marco demanded.

Cassie sighed. "I'm totally against this. But . . ."

"But? But? But what?"

Cassie turned to me. "Ax, is it possible to acquire DNA from blood alone?"

<Yes. It should be.>

"Blood?" Rachel made a face. "We're gonna get this guy's blood? Not me, my friend. Hepatitis, HIV, uh-uh."

<Diseases cannot be transmitted during acquiring,> I said quickly. <The acquiring process absorbs only DNA, and that DNA is isolated, encapsulated within your own bloodstream in a super-low temperature — and thus very stable — naltron molecule sphere. You see —>

"I think my brain just fell asleep," Marco interrupted. "So, okay, the blood is safe for us. So, Cassie, how do we get it?"

Cassie explained.

All the other humans, even Tobias, said "gross." They said "gross" very loudly and repeatedly.

I've learned something from my time with humans. When they say something is gross, they are almost always right.

CHAPTER 8

"So how do I acquire it without it acquiring me at the same time?" Prince Jake asked nervously.

"Don't be a big baby," Marco said. "Like you've never been bitten by a mosquito?"

"Never in cold blood," Prince Jake said.

It was several days later. My human friends attend school five days in a row, then do not attend for two days. They don't know why. But they try and arrange for missions to take place on non-school days.

We were in the barn, surrounding a transparent glass box. In the box were a number of small, fragile-looking flying insects.

"You need to catch one in your hand. Don't

squeeze too hard or you'll kill it," Cassie said. "Like this." She stuck her hand in the box. After two unsuccessful attempts, she enclosed a mosquito in her hand.

She withdrew her hand, covered the box again, and began to focus on the mosquito. After a moment she opened her eyes. "Okay, who's next?"

"Just hand me your mosquito," Marco said. "It probably already bit you, so maybe it's not hungry anymore."

"We can't all morph the same mosquito," Cassie said. "Only females suck blood. Males are useless."

"Amen," Rachel said, then laughed.

"So what's that mosquito in your hand?" Marco demanded.

"Like I know?" Cassie said. "I don't have a magnifying glass that good. And even if I did, how exactly do you tell a male from a female?"

"That's easy," Marco said. "The males think loud belching is funny and the females don't."

"Is there *any* chance we could just get on with this?" Prince Jake asked.

<Yes,> I said. <I do not fear the bite of these tiny insects.> I put my hand inside the glass cage. I had some difficulty grabbing one of the creatures, though. Human hands are stronger and faster than Andalite hands. In the end, Cassie grabbed a mosquito and handed it to me.

<Thank you,> I said, and began to acquire the necessary DNA.

When we had all finished Prince Jake said, “Okay. Let’s go.”

We morphed to birds of prey to fly quickly to the hospital. With harrier eyes I saw that the human Hewlett Aldershot the Third was still in his hospital bed. But there was a major difference. There were now four large humans seated around him. In the room next door to the left, we saw four more. And in the room next door to the right, another four.

Human-Controllers, no doubt. And no doubt heavily armed. Twelve armed humans to protect Hewlett Aldershot the Third from us.

<Kind of flattering, actually,> Rachel said. <Twelve guys? And maybe more we don’t see.>

<The Yeerks must have some high-ranking people in this hospital,> Cassie observed. <To get two private rooms just for guards like that?>

<So how do we get in?> Marco wondered.

<How about a diversion?> Rachel suggested. <I go into elephant morph, Jake does his rhinoceros, and we rip that place apart!>

I said, <As I understand, we each hope to bite the human, so that we can be reasonably sure of extracting sufficient blood. But Rachel, before you can go from elephant to mosquito you must pass through human. I, on the other hand, have

no need of an intermediate stage. And nothing would draw the attention of a bunch of Controllers better than an Andalite.>

It made perfect sense. Prince Jake agreed that it made sense. So while the others went up to the roof and morphed back to human in preparation for becoming mosquitoes, I landed in a dark, open window at the far end of the hospital.

I fluttered inside, waited, listening. I heard human breathing. My harrier eyes adjusted to the darkness and I could make out a young human female, looking very frail in her bed.

I demorphed as quickly as I could, shedding feathers and growing fur.

Suddenly the girl's eyes opened.

"Who are you?" she demanded. "Are you a fairy?"

<No. I am an Andalite.> It was all I could think of to say. Besides, I felt reluctant to lie to a sick child.

"What's your name?"

<My name is Aximili-Esgarrouth-Isthill.>

"That's a funny name," she said. Then she closed her eyes and began to sleep once more.

I took a deep breath. I moved to the door as silently as I could. I opened it and stuck one stalk eye out into the hall. Two humans in white were at the far end of the hall.

I took another deep breath. *Well,* I thought, *I* am *supposed to create a diversion.*

I opened the door and stepped out into the hallway. The two humans did not see me till I had nearly reached them. Then their mouths opened very wide. And their faces began to change color: one turned white, the other red.

I don't know why.

"Holy . . ."

"What the . . ."

Obviously they were not Controllers or they would have been yelling "Andalite!" rather than "Holy" and "What the." These were innocent humans.

<Hello,> I said. <Please, do not be alarmed.>

"It's . . . it's some weird, mutated deer!"

"It's some kind of trick. It's gotta be a trick. All right, Terry, you can come out now. Hah-hah, big laugh."

I passed them by and kept walking toward the heavily guarded room of Hewlett Aldershot the Third.

A human went past pushing a cart loaded with food on trays. He never looked up. He just kept looking down as he went. Then I guess he noticed my hooves.

"Aaaahhhh!" he cried, and shoved the cart so hard it turned over.

Clang-clash-WHAM!

Thus began the diversion. Suddenly doors opened. Heads stuck out and looked and screamed. People came running down the hall. Most turned around when they saw me and ran the other way.

"Oh, no! Did you see it? Did you *see* it?"

"It's a monster!"

"I *knew* they were doing genetic experiments down in the labs! It's some kind of freak!"

It would almost have been insulting, if I were sensitive.

But then the door to the right of Aldershot's room opened. Out stepped a human. He gaped at me for a second, then yelled, "Andalite!"

He gaped one second too long. He yanked out a gun. I snapped my tail forward and he quickly dropped the gun.

"Andalite!" he screamed again, but with extra hatred this time.

Now the guards came boiling out of all three rooms. They jammed into the hallway, too many to move freely. Human guns were being drawn. And I saw a couple of handheld Yeerk Dracon beam weapons, too.

In a split second they would all start shooting. The lead slugs from the human weapons would be most dangerous. Not just to me, but because they would rip through the walls and might hit innocent people.

"Shoot! Shoot him, you fools, or Visser Three will have us for lunch!" one of the humans roared.

FWAPP!

I whipped my tail, left to right, a millimeter from slicing open the front row. They backed up, stumbling back into their fellows.

FWAPP!

I whipped again, but now they were ready to start fighting. And I was seriously outnumbered and worried about innocent humans being hurt.

Obviously, I had not planned the diversion very well.

And that's when it occurred to me. The one way to keep from getting shot.

<I surrender!> I cried. <I want to defect.>

CHAPTER 9

"What?"

<I wish to defect. I am interested in joining the Yeerks. I would like to become a Controller. Do you have any information on membership? Is there a fee?>

A dozen weapons were leveled at me. From behind me, at that end of the hall I heard other human voices.

"What is going on around this place?"

"Is that a horse?"

"Look at the eyes on its head!"

"Where's security?"

The leader of the Controllers made a snap decision. He hustled me out of the hallway and into the room where Hewlett Aldershot the Third was sleeping his comatose sleep.

The room was small. Too small for all the guards. There were only five of them now. Much better odds.

"You want to join us?" one of the Controllers asked dubiously.

<Actually, no,> I said regretfully.

FWAPP!

I struck and the nearest guard leaped back, plowing into his men. I had about half a second before they'd recover and shoot.

FWAPP! CRASH!

I shattered the window with my tail blade.

<Here's a trick I learned from Visser Three!> I yelled. I ran three steps, ducked my upper body, flattened my stalk eyes, tucked my legs, and flew through the shattered window.

Down I fell!

<Yaaahhhh!>

Too far, way too far, but better than getting shot.

<The window's open, Prince Jake!> I cried. <And the Controllers are —>

WHAM!

CRUNCH!

<— distracted.>

I landed in a bush that cushioned some of my

fall but also tripped me. I rolled and tried to scramble up, but then realized, as ridiculous as it seemed, that I was trapped inside the prickly, clawing branches of the bush.

Blam! Blam! BlamBlamBlam!

The guards were firing from the window. Bullets tore the branches and slammed into the damp soil all around me.

Human weapons operate on a principle of exploding gases that drive a solid metal pellet along a tube. The tube acts to spin the bullet, thus improving accuracy. It's no Yeerk Dracon beam, or Andalite Shredder, but it does a very good job of blowing large, messy holes in you.

I needed to get small. Small enough to get away!

I began to morph the mosquito.

<We're in!> I heard Prince Jake say. <Ax, are you okay? We think we hear gunshots, but our hearing in these morphs is fuzzy.>

<You are correct: You *are* hearing gunfire,> I said tersely.

<Are you okay?> Tobias asked.

<Not really. But I hope to be soon.> *If I live that long,* I added silently.

I was shrinking rapidly, and now there were sirens wailing at a distance, coming closer.

"Police!" I heard a human voice cry from above. "We can't get arrested."

"If we let the Andalite escape we'll get worse than arrested! Keep shooting!"

"I can't see what I'm shooting at. The bushes. And it's all in shadow."

I was shrinking faster. Leaves that had seemed quite small now were as big as my face. Branches that were twisted and tiny were growing larger, larger. They no longer trapped me. I could have walked out of the bush, except for the fact that my legs were dwindling even faster than the rest of me.

Someday Andalite scientists will find a way to make the morphing technology totally predictable and logical. But for now it is often erratic, weird, and totally illogical. Especially when morphing bizarre Earth animals.

My hind legs had finished shrinking when they were still as big as an Earth cat's legs. Then they began to reverse and grow again. My hind legs thinned, becoming mere sticks, but their length became ridiculous. Longer than the rest of me all together!

My front legs became somewhat shorter stick legs and a third pair grew from my arms.

I was no longer on all fours. I was on all sixes. I was standing on insect legs, yet most of my body was still Andalite. A very small Andalite, but far too large to move around on insect legs.

My stalk eyes crawled forward across my

head, down to a point just above my main eyes. They began to extrude. They grew like some horrible fast-sprouting tree. A long, bare stick that then sprouted new branches: short, stunted, twisted branches. Bulging round pods popped from my head at the base of these hairy sticks — these antennae — and began to move them around.

My main eyes were still functioning, but from the antennae I received a whole onslaught of new sensory input. Temperature! Wind direction! Sound waves from the rustling leaves, from the muddy, far-off voices, and sharp, disturbing sounds from the explosions of gunpowder and the impact thud of massive bullets all around me.

I was no longer worried much about the bullets. I was too small to hit except by the most amazingly unlucky shot. I was less than an inch long and getting smaller.

The dirt looked like a field strewn with boulders. The trunks of the bushes sprouting up from the ground were thicker and taller than any tree on Earth or my planet.

My nostril slits closed and began to twist and push outward. Two stubby, hairy palps appeared, and these immediately began feeding an entirely new set of data to my brain.

Smell! But not smell as an Andalite or human

knows it. This was specific, targeted, directed smell. It wasn't smell that waits passively for whatever comes along. The palps were searching the molecules of the breeze, sampling, looking . . .

Hungry.

Gossamer wings rose from the melting flesh on my back. My body pinched into three distinct segments: a tiny head, a muscular thorax, and a swollen, vast abdomen. Overlapping armored plates clanked down the bottom of my abdomen.

And yet, through all this, a tiny, shrunken version of my Andalite main eyes continued to function.

I wish they hadn't. I wish I'd never had to see what happened next.

From my chin, from the place where a human would have had a mouth, it grew. A spear! A needle! Impossibly long. On the end were tiny, serrated teeth, almost like the teeth of a saw.

Inside the spear it was hollow. It was a straw. A tube for sucking blood.

A retractable sheath grew along with the spear. A sheath that would help keep the needle sharp.

Blood.

That was my goal. That was my hunger.

Blood!

I fired my gossamer wings and rose, unsteady and wild, upward, upward, to where my palps had located the scent they sought: the sweet scent of exhaled animal breath. The guidepost that pointed the way to food.

CHAPTER 10

That's when my eyes stopped working. I was blind for a few seconds as the morph completed. I shrank some more, and suddenly from my forehead popped two bulging compound eyes.

Through them I saw a vision of reality shattered into thousands of tiny pictures. Thousands of tiny pictures, each different from the next, each a fragment of distorted light and eerie colors and nightmarish swirls of energy.

I never lost control of the morph. I mean, I never forgot who I was, or what I was, as sometimes happens in a morph you're doing for the first time.

So it wasn't that I lost my mind. It was simply that the hunger of the mosquito was so great, so powerful, so totally clear and forceful, that I felt myself going along with it. Accepting it.

I was flying, and knowing who I was, and yet as the mosquito's instincts cried, "Blood! Blood!" I answered, "Yes! Yes!"

Mosquitoes do not fly with the speed and acrobatic genius of a fly. Or with the precision and power of a bird. They fly wildly, blown by chance breezes. The legs dangle long and drag at the air. The wings are underpowered. But the mosquito gets where it's going.

It seems a harmless insect when you see it. But I have done some research. Mosquitoes transmit bacteria, viruses, and parasites. They carry the diseases encephalitis, yellow fever, and malaria.

Malaria alone kills two million humans each year. Mosquitoes are the greatest mass murderers on planet Earth.

<Ax! Ax! Talk to me,> Prince Jake called, and I realized suddenly that he'd been yelling for some time.

<I am fine,> I said. <I have morphed to mosquito.>

<Good,> he said. <Look, I know what you're feeling right now. Don't fight it. The hunger stops once you bite.>

<Follow the smell,> Cassie said. <That's carbon dioxide your palps are smelling. It comes off animals, including humans. Go for it.>

I rose, hungry, to the open window. But there I was confused. There were many warm, carbon dioxide-emitting creatures.

The one I was looking for was lying down. Lying still. I focused on the mosquito senses. I struggled to put together the sound waves from my antennae, the smell of carbon dioxide from my palps, and the shattered, lurid view through my compound eyes.

Huge, huge, vast beyond imagining, stretched my target. Hundreds of times my length, millions of times my weight, Hewlett Aldershot the Third lay prone, oozing attractive aromas.

I fluttered on gossamer wings and landed. I was on a rough, uneven surface. There were bumps and ridges of warm, pink flesh. Here and there, like lone trees scattered on a dry plain, hairs rose like curved spears from the flesh.

The flesh was alive. It moved slightly, causing me to rise and fall. The human was breathing. But more fascinating than the slow rise and fall of breath, was the Thump! Thump! Thump! of a drumbeat beneath my feet.

A pulse. The beating pulse of blood rushing through arteries and veins.

And then . . .

POP!

CHAPTER 11

There was a distinct popping sound and suddenly, instantly, I was no longer a mosquito tapping into a human's vein.

I was in space. White, empty Zero-space!

<Whaa . . . ? What? Z-space?> I cried. Maybe not the most brilliant comment. But I was confused.

I kicked my legs instinctively. My Andalite legs. I was back in my own body. But there was nothing to kick against.

I felt no sensation of movement, no air was rushing over me. Already the lack of oxygen was beginning to cloud my brain. My eyes were going blind. My limbs were numb.

Zero-space! It was impossible. And yet here I was.

I looked around frantically. I turned my stalk eyes in every direction. I saw my own body, inside and out. An *n*-dimensional jigsaw puzzle, twisted so that I could see inside my own body.

And there, to one side of me, were four human bodies spread out in the same way — weird cross sections. I saw Prince Jake's face, but also his beating heart and the muscle tissues of his legs and the inside of his brain. The same with the others.

They were all writhing in agony.

And there was one bird, very still.

<Prince Jake! Tobias!> I cried. But of course they couldn't answer. There was no air to carry their mouth-sounds. There was nothing, not even the few stray atoms and molecules that float free in regular space. There were no stars or planets. Nothing exists in Zero-space.

I happened to catch sight of a silvery, graceful creation, perhaps half a mile away. A ship! As with the bodies, I saw the inside and outside of the ship all in one picture. I could see distorted individuals inside, going about their duties.

But even mind-numb and gaping at a confused nightmare vision, I knew what sort of creatures they were.

Andalites. It was an Andalite ship!

Its Zero-space engines burned brightly, but it was not moving away.

It hit me in a flash. I knew what had happened. As any Andalite knows, when you morph something much smaller than your own body, the excess mass is extruded into Zero-space. It hangs there, a wad of randomly arranged matter.

Or at least that *was* the theory. There was nothing random here. Because we were outside of normal three-dimensional space, I could see the insides of everything and everyone. But the bodies were still definitely human and Andalite bodies. They were not just random globs.

Once, some time ago, I explained to my human friends about excess mass being pushed into Zero-space. They asked whether some ship traveling through Zero-space might not hit these matter bubbles.

I'd laughed. After all, the odds were . . .

Well, obviously it now seemed the odds were pretty good. The Andalite ship had come too close and had pulled us into its magnetic field. It was now dragging us in its wake as it blasted through Z-space.

<Aboard the Andalite ship!> I cried with all the power I could still muster. <Andalite ship! Andalite ship! We're trapped in your wake and dying. Help! Andalite ship, help!>

The energy it took to cry out sapped my remaining strength. There was no air. I could literally see my own lungs collapsing inside me. I could see my hearts frantically beating, trying to keep me alive.

But now the hearts were slowing . . . slowing.

<Andalite ship! Help! Help!> I cried. <Help . . .>

I can't describe the pain of seeing my own fellow Andalites so close. The first Andalites I'd seen in so, so long.

But of course they couldn't see me. Inside the ship they preserved normal three-dimensional space. The Andalites in the ship saw only bulkheads and decks about them.

And then I literally saw, as though I were standing outside myself, the last beats of my heart. I saw the blood flow in my brain slow and stop.

I knew I was going to die. I was going to die within sight of my own people.

Die . . .

My consciousness went dark.

And then suddenly, I wasn't dead. I wasn't spread out in multiple dimensions. I was in one piece, alive, and lying on my side on a shaped table that adjusted gently to hold my tail and legs comfortably.

<What?> I said, for no particular reason.

<I don't think *what* is the question,> an Andalite voice said. <I think *why* and *how* and especially *who* are the questions.>

I turned my stalk eyes and there, standing beside me, were three Andalite warriors.

CHAPTER 12

<I am *Aristh* Aximili-Esgarrouth-Isthill,> I said.

<Prince Elfangor's little brother?> one of the Andalites blurted.

<Yes. I am Elfangor's brother.> I sighed a little at that. I know it's ridiculous, but as much as I loved and admired Elfangor, it did get annoying always being called "Elfangor's little brother."

They were three Andalite warriors. You could tell they were warriors by the way they carried themselves. By the way they managed to look totally straight and stiff, and yet had just a little bit of a casual slouch in their hind legs.

That, plus the fact that each had a military-

issue Shredder weapon and extra power cells slung on a bandolier.

<I am Samilin-Corrath-Gahar, captain of this ship,> the oldest of them said. <My tactical officer Hareli-Frodlin-Sirinial, and our ship's physician, Doctor Coaldwin-Ashul-Tahaylik. Now what in *yaolin* are you doing drifting around in Zero-space with five aliens?>

<Did you save them? Are they safe? The aliens, I mean?>

Doctor Coaldwin answered. <Yes, they are quite well. But what unusual physiology! Four of them are clearly bipedal but lack any sort of tail. They walk on two legs and manage to do so without having a tail for balance. Quite fascinating. The remaining alien is evidently designed for flight and —>

<Yes, thank you, Doctor,> Captain Samilin interrupted. <The question for the *aristh* is what was he doing in Zero-space in the company of these . . . these fascinating aliens.>

I climbed to my feet. I felt shaky, but I couldn't just lie there. <Captain, I was in morph. In a very small morph. Then I heard a popping sound and suddenly I was in Z-space.>

<What? You are the extruded mass from a low-mass morph? It's impossible!> the doctor cried, his eyes bright with excitement. <I mean, it's not impossible, perhaps, but it's never hap-

pened. This will annihilate every existing theory of morph mass displacement. This will be a scientific breakthrough of —>

<Yes, no doubt,> the captain interrupted again, sounding more testy. <But as fascinating as it is scientifically, I have a bigger question. We know how you came to be floating in Zero-space, *Aristh* Aximili, but how did these aliens arrive here, since only Andalites possess the morphing power?>

It was a direct question from a superior officer. A *very* superior officer. A ship's captain is lord and master of his ship. An *aristh* is basically something a ship's captain might scrape off his hoof.

Even though the captain's tone was very accusatory, I had this sudden urge to start laughing. It was sheer relief. First, because my friends were well. But also because I was back among Andalites.

They looked like me. They spoke like me. They moved like me. I wanted to laugh and to be sad.

<Answer the captain's question!> the tactical officer roared, speaking up for the first time. As the number two officer, tactical officers are the ship disciplinarians.

<Sorry, sir,> I said. <It's just that I haven't seen a fellow Andalite in a very long time. And I

thought I might never . . . that I might be stuck on Earth for the rest of my life.>

The T.O.'s fierce expression softened. But not much.

The captain nodded and said, <Just give me your report, *Aristh*.> But he said it nicely.

<Yes, Captain. I have been marooned on Earth for approximately point seven standard Andalite years. I believe I am the only survivor following a battle between the Dome ship where I served and a Yeerk Pool ship. The Pool ship was assisted by a concealed Blade ship belonging to Visser Three.>

The T.O. made a sneering, disgusted sound.

<The Dome was separated prior to battle and . . . I was in the dome. It wasn't by choice. I was *ordered* to the dome.> I felt foolish defending my actions. But I didn't want it to look like I was some kind of coward. <Anyway, the dome fell from orbit and crashed in one of Earth's oceans. I was down there underwater for several Earth weeks, until the humans came to rescue me.>

<The same humans who are now in sick bay?> the doctor asked.

<Yes.>

<They used some human diving craft?> the T.O. asked.

<No. They morphed into aquatic animals and rescued me.>

The captain showed no expression except a wary tightening around his main eyes. <They *morphed*. And where exactly did they acquire the ability to morph?>

This was going to be hard. Some time ago I had managed to make contact with the Andalite command. They had basically told me to take the blame for giving humans morphing ability. They didn't want to blacken Elfangor's reputation as a hero. Giving away morphing technology is a major crime.

What should I say? Should I lie to the captain? It seemed impossible. But I had orders from much higher sources.

<I did, sir. I gave them morphing capability.>

The captain just looked at me. <I see. You are not a good liar, *Aristh* Aximili.>

My hearts skipped a few beats. <Sir?>

The T.O. sighed. <You young fool, if *you* gave the morphing power to the humans, how did they manage to already be in morph the first time you saw them? Obviously, they were already capable of morphing by the time they discovered you.>

What could I say? I hadn't exactly had time to prepare a good story. I was supposed to be a mosquito a few billion miles away. Now I looked like a liar *and* an idiot.

I said nothing, just tried to stand at attention.

<Doctor, thank you,> the captain said, dismissing the doctor. <Perhaps you'd like to go check on your "humans." And see if you can't analyze this Zero-space problem young Aximili has discovered.>

The doctor left. The captain leaned close. <*Aristh* Aximili, I'd like to know why you're lying to me.>

<I would never lie unless . . .>

<Unless *what*, you insignificant *aristh*!> the T.O. cried. <You are addressing a ship's captain!>

I nodded. <Yes. I know.>

The T.O. started to yell again, but the captain cut him short with a raised hand.

<*Aristh*, have you at any time made contact with the home world during your time on Earth?>

<Yes, Captain,> I said, practically collapsing with relief. Captain Samilin got it. He understood.

<And were you given orders at that time?>

<Yes, Captain.>

He looked as if he might ask more, but he didn't. He looked at me for a long time. Then in a much gentler voice he said, <What happened to Elfangor?>

<He was killed. By Visser Three. On the planet surface.>

The captain nodded. The T.O. looked shocked.

<Prince Elfangor did this?> the T.O. asked in an awed voice. <Prince Elfangor broke the law of *Seerow's Kindness*?>

<That speculation will never leave this room,> the captain said harshly. <It was *Aristh* Aximili who foolishly gave the morphing power to the humans. But between us, I'll say this. I served under Prince Elfangor. I was his T.O. at one time. And anytime Elfangor did something, it was for a good reason.> He looked right at me and said, <Elfangor was my friend as well as my prince. I'll believe he broke the rules. I'll never believe he did wrong.>

CHAPTER 13

"Hey, I have a question," Marco said, raising his hand and waving it around in the air with a sense of urgency.

<What question?> I asked him.

"Where, where, where . . . WHERE ARE WE?"

<We are in the sick bay of the Andalite assault ship *Ascalin*.> I tried not to sound too happy about that fact. I knew my human friends would be devastated at learning they were marooned far from Earth.

"*Ascalin*? Isn't Ascalin that new salad green?" Rachel wondered.

<We have just come out of Zero-space and are now moving at top space-normal speed toward planet Leera.>

"Leera? Where the psychic frogs are from?" Cassie said. "The creatures who the Yeerks were going to use those mutated sharks on?"

<Yes.> As we already knew, the Yeerks were having difficulties invading Leera in their usual style. The Leerans' psychic abilities make them able to detect the presence of a Yeerk in another Leeran's head. The Yeerks were going to alter hammerhead sharks to make them suitable for Yeerk infestation, and then use those shark-Controllers as shock troops in the oceans of Leera.

"But we busted up that plan back on Earth," Marco said impatiently. "I was there, remember? I know this part. What I meant was, how did we end up here? One minute I'm a mosquito, then bim, bam, boom I'm my cute, lovable self again, only I'm looking up at some Andalite who's asking whether I ever had a tail! I almost peed myself. I thought he was Visser Three!"

<It seems our extruded mass was swept up in the wake of a passing ship. Everyone is very surprised and excited. We have made a scientific breakthrough.>

"Oh, good, I feel better already," Rachel said, using a tone humans call "sarcasm."

"So how do we get back?" Prince Jake asked.

<No one knows. The doctor and the other scientists on board are working on the theory. There

may be a snapback effect. But they don't know. And we are about to land on Leera. This is an assault ship, which means it carries a large number of surface attack craft. It is no longer a *secret* Yeerk invasion of Leera. It has become a major, open battle. They have four Pool ships in orbit and two Blade ships. Hundreds of Bug fighters. We have less than a third of their forces.>

"So let me get this straight," Rachel said. "Suddenly we're a bazillion miles from home and we're about to get dragged into a serious shooting war where the good guys are outnumbered three to one?"

<Yes,> I said.

"Cool," Rachel said. "What can we do to help?"

"Oh, even for you, Rachel, that is just sick," Marco said.

<You can do nothing,> I said. <I told you the *kafit* bird morph that Visser Three used is from my home planet. That means our side may be infiltrated by Yeerks or their allies. We can't trust your secret to anyone. If you do get back to Earth somehow, you won't survive if the Yeerks find out who you are.>

Cassie tilted her head and looked at me with a sad sort of smile. "If *you* get back to Earth? Meaning you won't be going back with us?"

I wished I hadn't used those words. My head was too full of problems and complications and every kind of emotion. I didn't really want to think about being separated from my human friends.

Rachel looked disgruntled. "I have news for you, Ax. If there's some Yeerk butt-kicking being done today, I'm in on it."

<We have to follow the captain's orders,> I said.

"Says who?" Marco asked.

I was beginning to feel still more troubling emotions. Something bordering on panic now. And, strangely enough, guilt. <I am just a lowly *aristh*. Like a human cadet. I have to follow orders.> I looked pleadingly at Prince Jake. <You have to understand. You are no longer my prince, now that I am back among my own people.>

They all looked at me. It wasn't a nice look.

Prince Jake tried not to seem bothered. But although I am no expert on human facial expressions, I believe my statement did cause him concern.

<Maybe you need to think about who your people are now,> Tobias said in a private whisper that no one else heard.

<I'm not you, Tobias. I'm not a *nothlit*. I'm not one species trapped in the body of another.>

<No. But I don't think you're just a lowly *aristh* anymore, either. And whether you like it or not, you're one of us.>

I didn't answer him. He was wrong. Instead I said, as gently as I could, <The captain has ordered that until the situation is stable, you must all remain here. In this room. Please do not attempt to move about the ship.>

CHAPTER 14

The *Ascalin* raced, engines wide-open, toward planet Leera. I watched from the bridge. For some reason the captain had called me there and seemed to want to keep me close by.

Maybe he was worried about me being too close to the humans. I don't know. I just know that an *aristh* doesn't usually stay on the bridge.

It was small, as battle bridges go. None of the wide-open spaces of a Dome ship bridge. There was good, hardy grass underfoot, though. And the latest in sensors and computers ringed the circular space, watched by half a dozen intensely focused warriors.

It was an honor to be there. It was exciting.

So why did I keep picturing my human friends sitting in the little room off the sick bay?

A tall, holographic display shimmered in the middle of the room. It showed the planet and the ships in nearby space. Yeerk ships in red, our ships in blue. There was a lot more red than blue.

By focusing my mind, I could see one of the new thought-speak displays. It transmits data directly to your brain. Very "cutting edge," as Marco would say.

I decided that I had no reason to feel guilty. I had been united with the humans when we were on Earth. That made sense. But now I was back among my own people. My true place was here.

On the thought-speak display I called up a detailed map of the situation on the ground.

Planet Leera was ninety-two percent covered by water. Eight percent land in a few scattered islands and one continent. The land battle would take place on the continent. Neither we nor the Yeerks had much capability underwater where the Leerans built their cities.

I could see several Leeran cities, usually built within forty or fifty miles of the continent or one of the islands.

Whoever — Yeerk or Andalite — ended up controlling the continent would effectively control the planet.

<What do you think of the tactical situation, *Aristh* Aximili?> the T.O. asked me.

It startled me. He sounded almost friendly. <I'm not an expert on —>

<I did not suppose you were,> he snapped. <I asked for an evaluation.>

<Yes, sir. The Yeerks are strong in orbit above the planet. I would say the odds favor them. But they don't want the battle to take place up here. Even if they beat us, they might be too badly damaged to be able to invade and hold the continent below from Leeran counterattack.>

<I see. If they fear the Leerans on the surface, why take the risk of engaging us and the Leerans together on the surface?>

I was out of things to say. Of course, the T.O. was right! I must sound like an idiot.

The T.O. turned one stalk eye to look at me. <Because, *Aristh* Aximili, the Yeerks understand that different species do not fight well together. We have one way of doing things. The Leerans a very different way. The Yeerks are united under one command; we and the Leerans are not.>

I noticed the captain looking thoughtfully at me and at his T.O. He seemed displeased.

<There's a lesson there, *Aristh*,> the T.O. said. <We Andalites are strongest when we fight alone.>

<Yes, sir.> I knew what he meant. He was

talking about the humans. And I really should just keep quiet. <And yet, with all due respect, it was my human friends and I who destroyed the Yeerks' attempt to create a species of ocean-going shock troops for use here on Leera. If the Yeerks had succeeded in that plan, the situation here today would be impossible.>

The T.O. looked angry. I didn't regret having spoken up, but I was waiting for him to —

<Dracon flashes!> a warrior at a sensor station called out. <We have Dracon flashes at the north end of the continent. Now Shredder flashes. The battle has begun.>

An instant later, a holographic Andalite head appeared in midair before us.

<Force Commander Prince Galuit-Enilon-Esgarrouth,> the T.O. said. <Attention!>

No one stood at attention except me. They all had things to do. You don't actually stand at attention if you're doing something.

In a calm thought-speak voice the holographic head said, <The action has begun on the continent. There are heavy Yeerk forces. Carry out plan seven four. To our Leeran allies: May your great god Cha-Ma-Mib smile on you this day. And to all Andalite warriors: The People expect that every warrior shall do his duty.>

The *Ascalin* decelerated, slowing as it dropped into the thick, humid atmosphere of Leera.

<Sir, what is my battle station?> I asked the T.O.

He laughed the grim laugh of a warrior going into battle. <For the bold *aristh* who made all this possible? You'd better stick with me.>

He and the captain exchanged a glance and a laugh. I didn't know whether to be embarrassed or proud. Mostly, I was just scared.

The continent loomed larger and larger. Most of it was lush and green, primarily jungle. Green like Earth's forests and jungles, but with wide swaths of some brilliant yellow vegetation, too.

The northern end of the continent was less fertile, more barren, probably colder. It was in one valley there that the battle was underway.

<Visual,> the captain ordered. <Magnification optimum.>

The hologram that had showed space now switched to a startlingly real picture of the valley. I could see Yeerk forces, mostly Hork-Bajir with a reserve of Taxxons and a scattering of Gedds, dug in on high ground around the west rim of the valley. They had erected massive force fields covering their back, thus forcing our forces and the Leerans to come at them head-on.

Our ground skimmers were racing across rock and through scattered trees, firing and being fired upon. A force of Leerans was on foot, scrabbling over the rocks almost unprotected to assault the Yeerks.

<You see why the Yeerks chose to fight here?> Captain Samilin said. <As the T.O. was saying, different species under different commands cannot function well together. You see? We waste our forces protecting the Leerans from being mowed down. And as a result, we are weak.>

<The *Ascalin* will turn that around,> the T.O. said confidently.

<Landing approach,> a warrior called out. Then . . . <Captain! Malfunction in the ground-approach guidance system!>

The captain looked perfectly calm. The T.O. swung his face toward the warrior who'd spoken.

<What?!> he roared.

<Sir, the controls are frozen. I've been locked out. Attempting to override. Override failing!>

The T.O. leaped to the console. His fingers flew across the fields and resonators. I saw his concentration as he made the mind-link with the system.

Then, with absolute horror on his face, he turned to the captain. <Captain! We are on approach to land behind Yeerk lines. We won't have a prayer!>

The captain walked calmly over to his T.O. And then . . .

FWAPP!

The captain whipped his tail blade like lightning. The blade hit the T.O. at the base of his tail.

T.O. Hareli's tail fell to the deck and twitched. Every warrior on the bridge froze, staring at the impossible sight.

The captain drew his Shredder and fired.

TSEEEWW! TSEEEWW!

Warriors fell to the deck, stunned unconscious. The air crackled with heat. Static electricity sizzled and danced in blue flame across bodies and equipment alike.

Only the bleeding, horrified T.O. was left conscious. A deliberate insult: He was no longer dangerous.

<Ah, my good *aristh*,> the captain said, holding the Shredder on me and taking the T.O.'s Shredder. <I don't want to take the chance of injuring you. Visser Four would be very upset if I injured the creatures who have been causing Visser Three such trouble on Earth. Vissers Three and Four are such close friends. Just remain calm. It will all be over in a moment. And you will all be . . . guests . . . of the Yeerk Empire.>

CHAPTER 15

I stood there like my hooves had been nailed to the deck. It wasn't possible! An Andalite ship's captain a traitor?

Or was he a Controller?

No one moved. The computer guided the *Ascalin* down, down to sweep slowly forward, just a few hundred feet above the rocky ground. In seconds we'd be down.

T.O. Harelin was bleeding profusely from his severed tail. But I knew he would rather die than live without a tail.

The humans! It hit me like a Dracon beam blast. My human friends were back in the sick bay. The captain knew their secret. In a matter of seconds, so would the entire Yeerk Empire. The news would flash to Visser Three. There would be no going home for them. Ever.

And Earth, like Leera, would fall to the Yeerks.

<Prince Jake! Tobias! Cassie! Marco! Rachel!> I cried in private thought-speak. <If one of you can hear me, you must escape! The captain is —>

<The captain is a dirtbag,> Marco's thought-speak voice said, startlingly clear and close.

<What? Where are you?>

<Oh, gee, Ax, we decided not to just sit in our room with our hands folded like good little girls and boys,> Rachel said. <Sorry.>

<Ax, we are on the bridge,> Prince Jake said. <We saw what happened. Or saw as well as we can in these morphs.>

<Prince Jake, it is absolutely vital that Captain Samilin be stopped!>

<We can't take him out,> Cassie said. <We would demorph too slowly. But I happen to be *on* the captain, and I can definitely distract him.>

The *Ascalin* was settling toward the ground. Through the front viewport I saw row after row of Hork-Bajir, all with weapons drawn, totally surrounding the landing area.

<Do it, Cassie,> I said grimly. <Distract him and I will do the rest. We have just seconds!>

I stared, riveted, as a flea too small to be seen became a flea too large to be ignored. It grew on the captain's back, larger, larger, with twisting, morphing features.

<What is —> the captain yelled in surprise.

FWAPP!

I struck! My tail blade whipped forward, aimed for Samilin's neck.

He jerked back, dodged. My blade hit his upper right front leg a glancing blow. All around the room flies and cockroaches no one had noticed began to grow as my human friends demorphed.

But now the captain swept his Shredder toward me and I struck again.

FWAPP!

The weapon flew from his hand and skittered across the deck.

It was the captain and I, tail to tail. We faced each other, each quivering with energy and focus, each waiting for the opening that would allow us to swing the killing tail slash.

I flashed on the scene with Visser Three. This was the second time I had gone tail to tail with an enemy. This time my foe would not escape.

TSEEEWWW!

T.O. Harelin! He had snatched up the fallen Shredder and fired. The captain sizzled, looked horrified, then disappeared.

<Computer!> the T.O. yelled. <Emergency override, switch controls to manual!>

WHAM!

Too late! The *Ascalin* hit the ground hard. I was thrown off my hooves. My human friends, all back in their own bodies now, went rolling and tumbling. Only the T.O. managed to stay on his feet.

<Computer, emergency liftoff!>

<Unable to comply,> the disembodied voice said. <There is severe main engine damage.>

I saw Harelin rock back on his hooves at this news. <Humans, remorph! The only way out of here is to be invisible. *Aristh*, you, too.>

<I'm not running away!>

<Yes, you are, *Aristh* Aximili-Esgarrouth-Isthill. You and the humans will escape and get word of this evil to the commander. That is an order.>

<But —>

<Do you *know* how to take an *order*?> he roared.

<Yes, sir.>

<Morph something small. I'll blow you out the emergency hatch. Get as far from the *Ascalin* as you can. You won't have much time. Do you hear me?>

I knew then what he was going to do. I knew he had no choice. He could not allow himself to be taken by the Yeerks. He could not allow any of the Andalites on board to be taken alive. And there was simply no way to escape this trap.

<Prince Jake, we all have to morph small.

Um . . . um . . . flies! Morph to flies, and fly up to the ceiling of the bridge. There's an escape hatch.>

I noticed Rachel looking at me with total disdain. Then she looked to Prince Jake. "What do we do?"

"What he said," Prince Jake said. "Do it."

I focused my own mind on the fly morph. I expected T.O. Harelin's face to reveal surprise or horror as I began to undergo the changes. After all, flies are pretty horrific even by Earth standards.

But the T.O. wasn't interested. He was staggering now from the loss of blood. And he was making an announcement that would be transmitted throughout the ship.

<To all warriors and crew of the *Ascalin*. This is the tactical officer. The captain is dead. We are surrounded. No chance of escape. Nothing to do now but inflict the maximum damage on the Yeerks. In three minutes I will begin firing all ship's weapons. The Shredder flashback will cause the ship to explode.>

He let this sink in for a moment.

<Perform the ritual of death, my friends. Thank you for your service to this ship. You die in the service of the People, defending freedom.>

I was shrinking rapidly. The deck was rushing up toward me. Insect legs and insect antennae sprouted from me. But I was Andalite, at one with every Andalite on the ship.

From all over the ship, a hundred thought-speak voices spoke the words of the ritual. I couldn't help but join them.

<I am the servant of the People,> I said. I should have bowed my head, but I no longer had a head that could bow. <I am the servant of my prince.> All over the ship I knew my fellow Andalites were raising their stalk eyes upward.

<I am the servant of honor,> I said, and heard the echo of all those strong voices. <My life is not my own, when the People have need of it. My life is given for the People, for my prince, and for my honor.>

I fired the fly's legs, started the wings beating, and flew up toward the escape hatch. I have never felt worse than I did at that moment. So many would die. And I would live.

<*Aristh?*> the T.O. said weakly.

<Yes?>

<Maybe I was wrong. Maybe different races can be stronger together. Go with your humans and prove me wrong.>

The escape hatch blew open before I could answer. A powerful rush of escaping air launched me out into the Leeran dusk.

<Jake . . . Prince Jake,> I said. <We must get as far away as we can.>

We flew, rolling and tumbling through the air, riding the strong breeze wherever it took us. When the *Ascalin* blew itself up, we were safe from the blast. And safe, too, from the thought-speak cries of a hundred dying heroes.

CHAPTER 16

<Okay. Now what?> Rachel said.

I didn't have an answer. I couldn't think. I just kept turning it over and over in my mind: An Andalite ship's captain had turned traitor. It was impossible. Because the more I thought about it, the more I realized he could not have been a Controller.

The *Ascalin* had been in space for weeks. In order for a Yeerk parasite to have lived in Captain Samilin's brain, it would have to have had Kandrona rays. There was no way for even the captain to conceal a portable Kandrona aboard the ship.

<I said . . . *now* what?> Rachel repeated.

<I don't know,> I said.

<Well, if you don't, who does?> she demanded. <What are we going to do? Fly around looking for the nearest Dumpster so we can see if there's a tasty pile of rotting fruit? Come on, we need a plan.>

<I . . . I . . . I don't know what to do.>

<We need to find a way home,> Marco said. <Obviously, thanks to Captain Benedict Arnold back there, this whole war is going bad on us. I didn't think the almighty Andalites did things like that. I thought it was just us poor, dumb, primitive humans who'd sell out to the bad guys.>

<How about everyone getting off Ax's back?> Tobias said.

<Yeah, poor Ax,> Rachel sneered. <He throws us over in a flash for his big deal captain who, oops, turns out to be a traitor.>

<Rachel, I don't think that's really fair,> Cassie argued.

<Fair? Fair?!> Marco yelled. <If it wasn't for us totally ignoring Ax and his precious captain, Ax would be dead back there along with —>

<I wish I were!> I cried. <I wish I were back there with them. I wish I had died with them.>

I had not intended to say that. And I did not mean it. Not really. I wanted to live. I felt terrible about it, but I wanted to live.

<Okay, everyone shut up,> Prince Jake said at last. <That was rough, what happened back

there. A lot of good guys just died. Everyone is hyped up. So let's just chill.>

He waited a few moments before going on. <Here's what we do. We keep flying till we're near the two-hour limit. We won't get far in these bodies, even with this breeze, but we want as much distance as we can get.>

We flew in silence, seeing the strange planet through the distorted compound eyes of flies, hearing almost nothing, smelling things we could not identify. We were alone in silence with our thoughts. And after a while I almost wished the yelling and accusations would start again.

It's a terrible thing, living when so many others have died. It's terrible because no matter what you do, a single thought keeps popping up in your head: I'm glad it wasn't me.

I was glad it wasn't me.

We landed amid a tumble of rocks that would hide us from view. We demorphed. From what I could recall of the display on board the *Ascalin*, we were in a no-person's land between the Yeerk and Andalite forces. The battle could sweep over us at any moment.

"Okay, I'm calm now," Rachel said as soon as she had emerged from the fly morph. "So now that I'm calm, same question: Now what?"

"What do you think about having Tobias take a look around?" Prince Jake asked me.

<I don't know,> I said.

Prince Jake looked at me with a narrowing of the eyes and pressing together of the lips. The expression is "annoyance," I believe.

"Tobias? Go up and take a quick look," Prince Jake said. Tobias flapped up from the ground. Prince Jake looked at me. "Now, listen up, Ax. I know you're feeling bad. For lots of reasons, probably. But you feeling bad doesn't let you off the hook."

<What hook?>

"Look, we got Andalites shooting at Yeerks. We have no humans in this fight except for us. Maybe you're not the big expert, but you know more than we know. So snap out of it."

Tobias circled overhead and came quickly back down to land somewhat painfully on a point of rock. <We have about a thousand heavily armed Hork-Bajir on one side, coming toward us fast. They're backed up by these kind of big, flat, oval ships flying maybe a quarter mile up and firing Dracon beams. Taxxons coming behind them. And over there, we have about two dozen Andalite ships, also low down, and maybe a hundred tough-looking Andalites on the ground. I may be wrong, but I don't think the good guys are gonna win this round.>

<We should try and reach the Andalite forces,> I said.

<Why, so some other Andalite traitor can rat us out?> Rachel said harshly.

My tail blade was at her throat before I knew it.

She stared at me with cool, blue human eyes. "What's the matter, Ax? Does the truth hurt? You blew us off so you could suck up to Captain Creep back there. If we go and find more Andalites, what happens? You tell us to go sit in a corner and be nice while you start yes, sir-ing and no, sir-ing the next Andalite you see?"

I pulled my tail blade back, horrified that I'd gotten so emotional. I felt the anger drain away. Rachel was right.

<I made a mistake trusting Captain Samilin. I made a mistake dismissing all of you. You have . . . you have kept me alive and befriended me for a long time. All I can say is that none of you knows what it's like to be completely cut off from your own people.>

<One of us does,> Tobias said quietly.

<All I can do is say I'm sorry. And I will consider Jake my prince until he says otherwise.> I turned to face Prince Jake, focusing all my eyes on him. <You are my prince until you, and only *you*, say otherwise.>

For once he did not say, "Don't call me prince."

Instead he said, "Fine. Now what I want to

know is this: Is there anyone on the Andalite side we can be totally sure of?"

It was a hurtful question. I felt the last of my pride melting away. <The commander. If he were a Yeerk spy, this entire battle would already be lost.>

"It looks pretty lost to me," Marco said bluntly.

<Force Commander Prince Galuit-Enilon-Esgarrouth lost his entire family to a Yeerk raid on an Andalite outpost. His entire family: wife and three children. They died rather than be captured. Their bodies were fed to the Taxxons. We can trust Prince Galuit.> I sighed. <And we probably *should* trust . . . no one else.>

CHAPTER 17

It sounded simple: Reach the Andalite forces. But it is a very dangerous thing, advancing toward a lot of angry, very dangerous, very heavily armed, very nervous warriors.

<The automated defensive grid will fire at anything in the air that comes too close,> I warned. <Anything. If it is more than a few feet above the ground the sensors will pick it up, target it, and fire.>

"This ground is too rough to walk over," Cassie said thoughtfully. "And it's getting dark. We could try smaller birds. The seagull morphs again. No, wait! Bats! Not as fast, but very agile. And with echolocation we can fly close to the ground even in the dark."

“To the bat morph, Robin!” Marco said, with cheerfulness that seemed totally out of place.

“We morph, then we fly, hugging the ground the whole way,” Jake said. “Once behind Andalite lines we try and figure out a way to reach this Prince Galuit.” He looked at me. “And whatever happens, we stay out of this battle till we reach Galuit. Understood?”

<Yes, Prince Jake.>

Prince Jake looked at me with an unsmiling mouth. Then he said, “Don’t call me prince,” and formed a small smile with his mouth parts.

<Yes, Prince Jake,> I said.

I had been in bat morph before, and after doing mosquito and fly morphs it seems almost normal. It has fur, for one thing. And I find fur very comforting, even when it is dark brown and very different from my own blue.

But bats are almost cripples on the ground. Bat legs are stunted and clumsy, and their front legs — or arms, whatever — are encumbered by leathery wings. Being unable to run is disturbing for any Andalite.

I focused on the bat, this strange creature from a strange planet so far away. I shrank, down and down as if I were falling. As if I might fall into one of the thousands of bubbles in the volcanic rock beneath me.

My front legs withered and left me almost facedown on the rock. My tail blade crinkled, like a burning leaf. The crinkling, withering worked its way up my tail.

I couldn't help but picture the tactical officer in those horrible moments after the captain had struck and cut away his tail. I hadn't liked T.O. Harelin. He seemed to me like too many older officers: full of prejudices and arrogance. But he had been a true Andalite. He had died a hero.

Now my hind legs began to shrink, staying perfectly symmetrical till they were quite small. Then, at the last moment, tiny claws replaced the hooves.

My arms moved back, rotating a few degrees around my body. My fingers elongated relative to the rest of the arm, which was shrinking. Skin began to grow in loose, gray-then-black folds. It hung down from my arms as if I were wearing very loose human clothing.

Clothing is pliable fabric designed to cover the human body. Sometimes as protection against the cold. But mostly, as I understand it, because humans believe much of their body to be unacceptable. They are right, of course, but they cover all the wrong parts: There is nothing uglier than a human nose.

The loose-hanging skin tightened and be-

came wings. My ears grew larger. And of course, like almost all Earth creatures, I acquired a mouth.

I could see quite well. Not as well as a bird of prey, but almost as well as a human. But sight is not the special power of bats. The special power bats have is the ability to fire a series of ultrasonic sounds that bounce off solid objects and send back a sonic picture to the bats.

The Leeran sun was dropping fast. The bat eyes were already straining to see. But I had a perfectly clear picture of the rocks around me.

<Okay, let's go find this Andalite honcho,> Marco said.

I flapped my wings and flew. Once more in the company of my human friends.

I felt strangely at home. As though, despite Prince Jake's anger and Marco's sneering and Rachel's outright suspicion, I belonged with them.

For some reason at that moment, even with the images of death aboard the *Ascalin* fresh in my mind, I saw myself far away, in a very different body, eating delicious cinnamon buns with a mouth.

I wanted to be back there. I wanted to be back on Earth.

Captain Samilin had sold out to the Yeerks. Was I selling out to the humans?

CHAPTER 18

I flapped my leathery wings and fired my echolocation bursts and flew just inches above the rocks. The bat's echolocation sense created a sort of picture, like a sketchy line drawing, with edges all sharp and clear and surfaces just sort of scribbled in.

I dived between rocks, and rose just millimeters before hitting obstructions. I turned left, right, left in sudden, acrobatic jerks.

<This is insane!> Marco yelled.

Insane can mean several things when used by Marco. It can mean "stupid" or it can mean "fun." I think in this case it meant fun. Because as insane as it was, it was exhilarating.

<Yee-hah!> Rachel yelled, then laughed her feral, dangerous laugh.

Soon it was a sort of precarious game: How close could I fly to the jagged rock edges without ripping a wing or crushing my fragile bat bones in an impact?

And it took my mind off darker, muddier thoughts.

Then the exquisitely sensitive bat ears, the ears that could hear the echoes of hypersonic echolocation, heard something new. A hum. A vast, pulsating hum that grew and grew as we flew on.

<Prince Jake, I believe we are hearing the Andalite sensors,> I said.

<Oh, that's what that is?> Cassie remarked. <Almost like music.>

We flew on, low, occasionally scraping on jutting rocks. Then —

<Whoa! Pull up! *Pull up!*> Cassie cried. She was in the lead.

I shot upward.

TSEEEWWWW!

The blast of the Dracon beams and Shredders was deafening. The flashes were blinding to the bat's eyes. Hork-Bajir, twenty at least, were piling up against a group of three Andalites and two Leerans. The fighting was intense. It would be over in a few minutes.

It would be a slaughter. But Prince Jake had ordered us to stay out of it. And I would not abandon him and my human friends again.

And yet, a phalanx of Taxxons was moving in to finish off the wounded Andalites who had already fallen.

To my surprise, it was Cassie who said, <Jake, we should do something.>

<Didn't I say we had to stay out of the battles?> Prince Jake demanded.

<Yeah, that's what you said,> Tobias answered. <So what are we *really* going to do?>

Prince Jake hesitated. Then he said, <Okay, let's rescue them. Land, demorph, remorph, fast, fast, fast!>

But before we could land, the entire rock bowl where the Andalites and Leerans stood exploded.

Ka-BOOOM!

The shock wave sent me spinning through the air. I landed on my back, half-unconscious, deafened, blood in my eyes. And overhead the Yeerk ground attack fighter swept by to the hoarse cheering of the Hork-Bajir.

A huge, clawed foot landed inches from me. Hork-Bajir ran over me, stampeding in a forward rush, ignoring the tiny, winged creature that was me. They fired their Dracon beams steadily, yelling with triumph in their voices.

I heard no answering Andalite Shredders. The Yeerk forces were advancing. The Andalite line was broken.

<Prince Jake!> I called. <Tobias!>

<Get in the air!> Prince Jake yelled back to all of us. <Everyone who can fly, up! Get up!>

Could I fly? Yes! I rose from the ground just as the first wave of Taxxons came rushing forward.

Taxxons are huge, long worms. Like Earth centipedes, only much larger. Taxxons live in a state of eternal hunger. Desperate hunger. They will eat anything — dead or alive. Even their own fallen or injured brothers.

I fluttered past an open, questing Taxxon mouth. I saw a fellow bat, flying just a few feet above me. I saw it very clearly. And then, in an instant, it was gone. Simply gone.

<Where's Tobias?> Rachel cried.

<Tobias!> I cried. <He . . . he disappeared!>

<What do you mean, he *disappeared*?> Prince Jake demanded.

<I saw him. I was watching him. And he just disappeared.>

Now, twenty feet up, I could see more of the battlefield. The line of Hork-Bajir was already far ahead of us. Taxxons writhed across the dark landscape below.

If there were Andalites anywhere nearby, they had been destroyed. In my mind I pictured the tactical display aboard the *Ascalin*. I could see where we were and where the forces had been arrayed.

<We've lost,> I whispered, not sure if anyone even heard me. <We've lost.>

As if to confirm my grim realization, I saw the engine flares of a dozen or more distant Andalite ships rising from the surface of planet Leera. Rising, and running for their lives.

CHAPTER 19

We stood, in our own bodies, amid the filthy, reeking waste the Taxxons had left behind. We hadn't found Tobias.

Rachel was alternately crying and raging. Marco was sitting, silent. Cassie kept holding on to Prince Jake. And Prince Jake kept pulling away to pace, to mutter to himself, to wonder half-aloud what he should have done. What he could have done.

I stood off by myself. I couldn't help feeling that I was to blame. I was humiliated. I felt sick. I had turned away from my friends and trusted my own people instead. One of my own people had betrayed us. And the rest of my people . . .

well, they had probably fought well and bravely. But they had lost.

Just like the Hork-Bajir war. We had lost again, and condemned another race to slavery under the Yeerks.

And what a race! The Leerans were amphibians. They could travel in water or on land, although they built their cities underwater. But the terrifying thing was that the Leerans possessed limited but very real psychic powers.

Leeran-Controllers would be able to see past morphs and into the mind inside. It would be impossible to fool them for long. And if Leeran-Controllers were ever brought to Earth, their powers would soon reveal the truth of the Animorphs.

Not that the Animorphs would ever likely be able to return to Earth.

It was Cassie who shook me out of my dark thoughts. In a whisper she said, "Ax. I don't think Jake wants to have to ask you again, but what do you think we should do?"

<I don't know. We've lost. We're on a strange planet that will soon be under Yeerk domination. We've failed the Leerans, as we failed the Hork-Bajir. As we *are* failing the humans.>

Past Cassie's head I saw distant red flares from Yeerk ships dropping from orbit to land

more and more troops on the continent. Soon the continent would be an impregnable garrison of Yeerk forces.

"Tell me more about the Leerans," Cassie said.

I shrugged. <I don't really know any more than you know. They are amphibians. They live primarily in the oceans. Originally I suppose they came on land to lay their eggs. Now I suppose their technology allows them to do all that in their underwater cities.>

"So why do they even care about what happens on the land?"

<They wouldn't care. Except that the Yeerks can use the continent as a base for attacks against the underwater cities. Other than that, I don't suppose the Leerans would even . . . care . . . what . . .> I stopped breathing. Yes! Of course! Of course that would be Galuit's plan.

"What? What is it?" Cassie demanded sharply.

<Prince Jake!> I cried.

"Yeah?"

<We must reach the ocean. If I am right, some Andalites will be in the Leeran cities. In any case, we must get to the sea as quickly as possible!>

"Why?"

I hesitated. <Prince Jake . . . Jake . . . you

must trust me. We cannot stay on land. We have to reach the water.>

Prince Jake looked at me for a long time. "Okay," he said at last. "I trust you."

<One more thing,> I said. <If at any time it seems the Yeerks may catch us, if it seems they might take me alive, you must not let them. You must destroy me yourself rather than let them take me. Promise me.>

"*What?* Why?"

<Because I think I know what is going to happen. And if I am right, this defeat will become the greatest victory in Andalite history. And that information cannot fall into the hands of the Yeerks. No matter the price. No matter what.>

CHAPTER 20

The continent was small by continent standards, but it still took the rest of the night to reach the shore. We morphed birds and flew. We stopped when we were near the two-hour limit and rested. And all the while I wondered if there was enough time left.

We flew above scenes of recent carnage. Burned-out ground skimmers, crumpled Andalite fighters and Yeerk Bug fighters.

As the sun rose on Leera, I looked down and saw a still-smoldering Andalite ground attack ship crumpled into a Yeerk ship. They had hit so hard that you couldn't tell where one left off and the other began.

And then, finally, there was the sea. It

stretched forever, brilliant blue, far more vivid and bright than the oceans of Earth, which are usually gray.

I tried to look around and spot some landmark. Some outline of coastline that would seem familiar from my faint memory of the holographic maps. But it was just endless miles of muddy shallows, overgrown with rushes and reeds and strange yellow trees that swirled horizontally.

<Big ocean,> Rachel said. <How do we —>

<How do we what?> Prince Jake asked.

It took several seconds for us to notice, to realize.

Rachel was gone!

<Rachel!> Cassie cried. <Rachel!>

We searched the sky. Nothing. Not even our powerful raptor eyes could see anything. No clue. No sign. Nothing.

<What's happening?> Marco demanded, angry because he was afraid. <She was just here! She was talking!>

<Ax, what is this?> Prince Jake asked. <First Tobias, now Rachel!>

<I don't know. I don't know.>

<Maybe someone on the ground shot her,> Cassie moaned. <Oh, God, Rachel! Rachel!>

<There was no Dracon flash,> I said. <Nothing. One second she was there. The next second she was gone.>

<Maybe it was someone or something on the ground,> Prince Jake said. <We have to get out of here. Into the water!>

We dove from the sky. I knew no one had fired at us, but I dove as fast as the humans. Whatever was making my friends disappear, it scared me. Whatever it was, I didn't want to be in its sights.

Down we dove, wings back.

Splash!

I went under, plowing into the warm water. I instantly began to demorph. I bobbed to the surface, already more Andalite than harrier. The water saturated my feathers, but the feathers were disappearing. I sucked air in through a nasty hole that was part beak and part Andalite nose.

I dove under again, and finished demorphing. I surfaced and found Prince Jake, Cassie, and Marco all treading water, finishing their own demorphing.

"Dolphin morph!" Prince Jake said. "Ax, you'll have to morph your tiger shark."

"Wait, no!" Cassie said. "We don't know what's in this ocean, but the Yeerks thought hammerhead sharks would be the baddest things around, right? That's why they wanted to create shark-Controllers — to fight in this ocean. We should all go shark."

"Yeah. Good point," Jake agreed. "Okay, then. Let's go shark. And everyone watch everyone else. We've had two people disappear. We're not going to have a third!"

Shark, I thought, and began to perform the morph.

I should explain the Earth creatures called sharks. They are fish. They breathe by extracting oxygen from the water itself, using thin membranes called gills.

But there are many fish in Earth's oceans. Only a few are called sharks. Some sharks are pleasant, peaceful eaters of plankton. Others are small and prey only on smaller fish.

But there are some sharks that humans call "man-eaters." These sharks are swimming killing machines. If it is possible to imagine a Yeerk having its own natural body, a body perfectly adapted for the Yeerk's ruthlessness and destructiveness, the shark would be that body.

It has massively powerful jaws lined with razor-sharp teeth. It has skin that is literally covered in millions of very tiny teeth. Skin that can rip human flesh. And it has an array of senses each attuned to one thing: finding prey. Finding and killing.

Excellent eyesight. Excellent sense of smell that can detect a handful of blood molecules diluted in a billion gallons of salt water. An electrical field sensor that feels the energy of other living creatures.

If some scientist had sat down to design the ultimate seagoing predator, the ultimate seagoing biological weapon, and had come up with the hammerhead shark, he'd be very proud of his work.

I felt myself morphing the shark. Felt the scythelike dorsal fins grow from my spine. Felt my tail blade split to become the swept-back, skin-slicing tail. Felt my stalk eyes move out to the sides to become the ugly hammer's head. Felt the new senses come alive in my brain. Felt the teeth — the rows of serrated, triangular, flesh-ripping, bone-crunching teeth.

And I felt the shark's cold, clear, brutally focused mind join my own.

I kicked my tail and moved through the water. Jake, Cassie, and Marco swam beside me. I suppose, like me, they felt powerful at that moment. And would have felt more powerful still, except for one terrible reality: There should have been six of us.

And now only four sharks swam out into the Leeran ocean.

CHAPTER 21

<I wish Rachel and Tobias were seeing this,> Cassie said. Her thought-speak voice was a mix of wonder and bitterness. <This is nothing like Earth's oceans.>

It was true. The continent might have been a dull, uninteresting place, but the ocean was amazing. Earth's seas contain many fascinating and wonderful creatures, but most of what you see as you swim there is murky water and a sandy bottom.

In this ocean the water was as clear as air. Clearer, in fact, than Leeran air, which is so heavy with humidity it sometimes seems like you're breathing clouds.

The water was perfectly, utterly clear. We

were swimming in water that was forty feet deep, and we could see every detail on the ocean floor.

And what detail! Huge, billowing creatures like white and yellow sails, triangular with biological propellers at each corner. Brilliant, electric-blue worms or snakes, each seventy feet long, swimming in wild schools. A bizarre creature that rose and fell through the water by blowing air into a bladder so thin it was almost transparent. A wonderful sort of fish in the shape of a screw that rotated its way through the water.

And these creatures weren't scattered here and there, but everywhere. The Leeran ocean was a madhouse of life-forms.

Spread around across the ocean were bubbling chimneys of rock and soil, encrusted with squirming, writhing creatures, small and less small. My shark senses could feel the electrical discharge from these chimneys, and the intense warmth.

As I watched, a massive school of the brilliant blue worms came swirling around one of the chimneys. It swirled and my shark senses could feel the energy flow from the chimney into the worms.

<Look at that!> Cassie cried, excitement overcoming her sadness. <A thousand marine biologists could stay happy for a hundred years just studying this one small area. The animals. The

plants. The . . . the whatevers! I wish I knew more. I know this friend of my mom's who studies the ecology of coral reefs. She would cut off her arm to spend an hour here!>

<The creatures are feeding off the geothermal energy and electrical charge from these chimneys,> I said. <This may be an environment without predators.>

<It has predators,> Marco said darkly. <The Yeerks are here. And *we're* here. For now. Until suddenly we go "poof!" like Rachel and Tobias.>

That brought us all back to reality. Still, even afraid, even sad, even desperate, we could not ignore the wild, incredible scene all around us.

We glided, dark and deadly, through a peaceful sea. The Yeerks had been clever to consider using sharks to control this ocean. Wherever I looked I saw no razor teeth, no crushing jaws. Marco was right: There were predators here. But they were *us*.

And then . . .

<Hey, aren't those Leerans?> Prince Jake said. <Down and to the left.>

I looked. Yes, they looked like the one Leeran we had seen on Earth in the company of Visser One.

They were mostly yellow. They had skin that was slimy, as if covered with ooze, yet rough in texture, like gravel. They had large, webbed back legs. For arms they had four tentacles arrayed around their plump, barrel-shaped bodies.

The head was quite large, with a bulge at the back. It sat right on the shoulders. There was no neck. The face bulged outward and seemed to have just two features. A huge, wide, almost ridiculous mouth. And big, bulging eyes of a green that seemed almost to be lit from inside.

There were four Leerans. They were riding on water jets. The water jets were long, narrow tubes, flared in front to make a sort of wing, flared again in back to give extra maneuverability. Arrayed along the back wing were clusters of very narrow tubes pointed forward.

They had obviously spotted us and were coming toward us.

<Probably wondering what we are,> Cassie said cautiously. <They've never seen sharks.>

<These are the good guys, right?> Marco said. <I mean, these are the guys everyone's trying to save from the Yeerks.>

<Yes. Maybe we should contact them. They could lead us to the nearest Leeran city.>

<Do it,> Prince Jake said.

<Leerans!> I yelled. <Leerans! I am an Andalite in morph.>

Chuh-wooomp!

The spear flew through the water only slightly slower than a human bullet. I jerked left. Too late! The spear pierced my tail and kept on flying.

<Hey!> Marco yelled.

<I'm an Andalite! Andalite!> I cried. <Your friend! Your ally!>

<Aximili-Esgarrouth-Isthill and three humans from planet Earth. Not *our* allies,> a cold, thought-speak voice said. He laughed. <You have no secrets from these psychic Leeran minds.>

And suddenly the water boiled with the firing of a dozen spears.

Chuh-woomp! Chuh-wooomp!

This time we were more prepared. Still, we were not fast enough. A spear hit me in the side and stuck. Prince Jake avoided being hit, but Cassie was speared through and through. Marco was hit twice. Shark blood billowed.

The Leeran-Controllers laughed. <Die, Andalite! Die, humans! We'll carry your bodies to Visser Four!>

<Hey, great war! You can't tell who's on what side,> Marco yelled. <What is this, Vietnam?>

Three of us had been hit. But none of us was dead. The spears were fast, but very thin. No doubt they were deadly to Leerans or to other creatures of this gentle ocean.

But we were only hurt. Not crippled.

<We don't seem to be dead, just yet,> I said to the Leeran-Controllers.

The Leeran-Controllers gaped with their big green eyes.

<But . . . but the *haru-chin* spears are deadly!> one of the Leerans said. He sounded like he was pouting.

<Nah. Maybe around here they're deadly,> Prince Jake said. <But we're from a much tougher neighborhood.>

<Think it's true what they say about frogs?> Marco asked. <Think it's true that they taste like chicken?>

CHAPTER 22

We launched toward the Leeran-Controllers. Sharks are very fast in short bursts. Too fast for the shocked Yeerks inside the Leerans to react.

They tried to turn their water jets around. They were still trying when they were hit by four frustrated, scared, angry people in shark morph.

Andalites understand about tail fighting. But there is something very intimate and intimately violent about attacking with a mouth. You have to get very close. You smell and feel and touch your enemy.

We hit, mouths open. We hit, and in a flash the four Leeran-Controllers were off their water jets and trying to swim away.

They kicked their big hind legs, but they were

too slow. Using their psychic powers, they could feel our anger. It must have been terrible for them. It must have been terrifying.

I didn't care.

But then . . . I was rocked by a powerful psychic vision. A vision that cried out in despair and agony and desperate hope.

One of the Leerans had managed to squeeze out this plea for help. The Yeerk in his head was busy trying to stay alive, and the real Leeran had seized the moment to send this vision.

The picture that appeared in my head was grizzly and awful. But I knew it was real.

<Prince Jake! Bite their heads! Bite off the large lobe at the back!>

<What?> Cassie cried. <They're beaten already. I'm not going to kill them.>

I lunged for the nearest Leeran-Controller. The Yeerk in his head knew what I was doing, but when he tried to jerk aside I slapped him with my tail, stunning him.

I opened my mouth, then bit down hard on the lobe at the back of his head.

But what was most shocking to see was the Yeerk itself. It was ripped from the Leeran's head. The Yeerk writhed, helpless in the seawater.

<The Yeerks are positioned in their rear brain lobes,> I said. <Bite them off!>

<It will kill the Leerans!> Cassie said.

No, a strange voice said. *It will free us!*

It was four of us against the three remaining Leerans. It was short but brutal work. Four doomed Yeerks writhed, fatally out of place in the Leeran water.

Thank you! the Leerans said. It wasn't normal thought-speak. It was deeper than that. Images, ideas that appeared in our minds that we then translated into words.

<You need medical help,> Cassie said. <Maybe I could demorph and —>

No, we will be fine. We can regenerate most body parts. It will take some time and we will be weak, but there are caves nearby where we can rest and be safe. Thank you! Thank you!

I've experienced some strange events. But four bright yellow Leerans with half their heads removed actually thanking us was definitely one of the strangest.

<We need to reach the nearest Leeran city,> Prince Jake said. <Which way is it?>

It will be very difficult. In the last months the Yeerks have captured many of us and forced us to be Controllers. There are many like us between here and the City of Worms. You are powerful, but if even one Leeran-Controller encounters you and then escapes, your secret will be discovered.

<So how do we get there?> Prince Jake wondered aloud.

<Morph the Leerans,> I said.

Yes! the Leerans cried. *Yes, morph us. Take our water jets. As long as you stay away from other Leerans, you will be safe from psychic probing.*

Cassie said, <We don't like to —>

Yes, a Leeran responded, reading her thoughts. *You do not like to morph sentient creatures. You respect our freedom. But we offer you this freely. We have read what is in the mind of Aximili the Andalite. We know what he suspects, and we know that even among the Andalites there are traitors. So, friends, carry our DNA and help to free our people from the Yeerks.*

We rose to the surface. I demorphed. The humans demorphed. We lay there treading water, rising and falling on the gentle Leeran swells. The Leeran sun was still low on the horizon, coming up on another day. It turned the water golden around us.

I reached and pressed my hand against a Leeran's slimy yellow flesh.

Where sky meets sea, Andalite, human, and Leeran are joined as allies, my Leeran said. *Each with our weaknesses. Each with our strengths.*

It moved me somehow, as ludicrous as it might have looked to an outsider. Humans and an Andalite wallowing clumsily beside big, yellow "psychic frogs," as Marco called them. Three species on a world conquered by the Yeerks. We probably would have seemed pathetic to any Yeerk who happened to see us.

<A fellow Andalite told me we were weak because we are not united. We do not speak with one voice,> I said. <But this union does not feel weak.>

<Free people who get together to defend freedom are never weak.>

It was Marco who said that. Maybe you can see why, despite all their strangeness, I like humans. And I was starting to like Leerans.

We let the Leerans go their own way to their underwater caves to recover from their injuries.

And we began what might be the most bizarre morph any of us has ever done. The physical part was strange, but no more disturbing than any number of Earth creatures I've morphed. The powerful webbed feet in back, the four sinuous tentacles, the neckless head were almost ordinary compared to the body of a fly or a cockroach.

It was the new sense that was stunning: the *psychic* sense. It wasn't that I could read every thought in the heads of Prince Jake and Cassie and Marco. But I could feel enough of their secrets to be embarrassed for them. And, of course, for myself. Because my own secrets, my vain little ideas, my pretensions were all open to them as well.

I could see so clearly that Marco was hoping for some news of his mother, Visser One. He wondered if she was here on Leera, if she had survived our last encounter.

I could see and feel Prince Jake's crushing weight of responsibility. The way he kept running things through in his mind, over and over again. Trying to figure out what had happened to Tobias and Rachel. Desperate to find a way to protect the rest of us.

And I could feel Cassie's mind as she cried for Rachel and Tobias. As she wondered whether we were doing the right thing. As she dealt with the aftereffects of the violence we'd just endured.

<Well,> Marco said, obviously uncomfortable. <I would just like you all to know that whatever thoughts of mine you're reading are totally made up. They aren't real.>

<Same here,> Prince Jake said quickly. <Absolutely.>

<Hey,> Cassie said, <these are just morphs to us, right? Lots of times we have trouble controlling the brain of the morph. But we usually handle it. So maybe —>

<Maybe since these are just morphs to us,

maybe we can turn *off* the psychic thing!> Marco said, clutching at the idea.

Then, one by one, I felt their minds close to me. And I closed my own.

It seemed suddenly very lonely as we grabbed the water jets and rode away through the brilliantly alive sea. Suddenly very lonely.

But I guess each species feels most comfortable when they are just themselves. And for humans and Andalites, secrets and lies and the loneliness of privacy are natural.

CHAPTER 23

We passed though a loose ring of Leeran-Controllers set up around the far edges of the City of Worms. None challenged us. We were riding Yeerk-issued water jets, and we stayed far enough off that no one could read our thoughts.

The Leeran city rose from the seabed like a wondrous tower, perhaps half a thousand feet wide at its base, dwindling to a few dozen feet at the very top. The top pressed right against the sparkling water ceiling, up to the border between sea and sky. At the very top, huge fans sucked in air and blew out exhaust from the entire city.

The city itself violated every logical law, at least as far as Andalites or humans were concerned. Andalites and humans are accustomed to moving in two dimensions, left and right, forward and back. But in the water, up and down were just as likely as left or right.

<It looks like a gigantic Dairy Queen cone, poked full of a million holes,> Cassie said. <Look! Doors everywhere. Windows and doors all the same.>

The predominant color was pink. But there was blue and green and purple as well, in vast swatches of seemingly random color. Openings were everywhere. Leerans drifted in and out and around and through, a hundred feet up, twenty feet below us, everywhere.

And like some slow-motion tornado, the long, electric-blue worms swam around and around the City of Worms. They formed an eerie halo.

Even as strangers, we could tell the city was tense. There were weapons poking from many of the windows. And nestled up against the base of the city, floating free, were two craft I'd seen only in pictures: Andalite submarines.

<Are those good guys or bad guys?> Prince Jake asked, gazing at the submarines.

<Or a little of each?> Marco asked dryly.

<They are Andalite vessels,> I said.

<Let's go say hello,> Prince Jake said.

We swam toward the submarines. As we got nearer we could see that a transparent tunnel had been set up between the subs and the city.

Andalite warriors were rushing through the tunnel on urgent errands, their tails cocked and ready.

Down we went, sifting air from the water with our Leeran skin. Down we went, expecting at any moment to be challenged, even shot. But we passed through dozens of Leerans who made no move to stop us.

<It's the psychic thing,> Cassie said. <They *know* who we are and why we're here.>

<Then I guess they know who we're looking for,> Prince Jake said.

And to my amazement, an answer came. It was a vision that filled my head: a sort of arrow showing a doorway we should enter.

<Ooookay,> Marco said. <I guess we follow the yellow brick road.>

We entered the city through one of the thousands of windows. I don't know what I expected inside, but it wasn't what I found. The tower was merely a shell. Inside were seven or eight, maybe more, huge, floating, transparent bubbles. In each bubble there were levels, a dozen or more floors. There were open holes in the bottoms of the bubbles. Some seemed to be filled with water. Others were filled with air. All contained Leerans doing work, sleeping, living. And one, mostly air, contained perhaps two dozen Andalites on one floor.

We entered the bubble from the bottom and stepped out at last onto dry ground. Two Andalite warriors were waiting.

<Demorph,> one said curtly. <The Leerans have told us who you are. Commander Galuit is waiting.>

<So humility is just not something you Andalites do, is it?> Marco asked.

We demorphed. It felt good to be Andalite again. But I was worried. I was nervous. I had given my word to Prince Jake that he, and only he, would decide whose orders I should obey. It had seemed easy to make that promise before. But now we were going to see Galuit! The idea of saying no to *him* . . . it made me gasp.

We rushed and stumbled to the room where Galuit waited. Only he wasn't waiting. He was rushing forward to meet us. He was flanked by three tough-looking Andalite security guards, and accompanied by his aide, an Andalite who had lost one stalk eye and half his face from a war injury.

<*Aristh* Aximili,> Galuit said without bothering to introduce himself.

<Yes, sir, I —>

<No time,> he said with a dismissive wave of his hand. <I'm a member of the highest circles, so I know all about your escapades on Earth. Yours *and* Elfangor's. Very disappointed in Elfan-

gor. Although, by the galaxy, your brother could fight! I don't know how you came to be here with these humans of yours, but it is a stroke of luck! We need you.>

I was almost completely bowled over. First of all, Galuit even knowing my name was incredible. It would be as if a human child were sitting at home by the telephone and suddenly got a call from the head general of the army.

Second, Galuit needed me? *Needed? Me?*

<Sir, may I introduce this human named Jake?>

<I said I need you. Now stand to attention and listen to my —>

<Sir, this is Jake. My prince.>

That stopped Galuit in mid-yell. The guards all stared incredulously at Prince Jake. Then at me. Then at Marco and Cassie, as if they might be able to explain.

<Every warrior must have a prince to follow, and the princes must obey the People,> I said.

Galuit looked like he was seriously considering using his old tail on me. But then he nodded stiffly. <Just so, *Aristh*. No one is a law unto themselves. We each must serve.>

Galuit turned to speak to Prince Jake. <I have need of you to save this planet from the Yeerks. Will you —>

<Yes,> Prince Jake said.

<You say yes without knowing what I'm asking.>

<Will it save the Leerans? Will it keep them free? And most of all, will it hurt the Yeerks?>

<Yes to all three. Especially the last. If we save Leera it may turn the tide of the war against the Yeerks.>

<Then we'll do it.>

Galuit seemed surprised. Maybe even impressed. In private thought-speak he said to me, <I have known worse princes than this one.>

CHAPTER 24

Galuit explained what he needed and why.

It was exactly what I had suspected. The reason we had to flee the land and take to the sea. The reason I could not risk being taken by the Yeerks: It had all been a trap.

A trap for the Yeerks.

<We knew the Yeerks would take the battle to the continent,> Galuit said. <And we thought it very likely they would defeat us there. So we had a backup plan. We have planted a series of quantum bombs around the continent. Our plan was to wait until the Yeerks had moved all their troops down to the continent, then explode the bombs.>

I nodded. <Yes, I suspected this.>

Prince Jake looked at me out of the corner of his eyes, then raised one eyebrow. It wasn't an angry look, as I interpret human expressions. It was a little reproachful, though.

We had transferred to one of the submarines and were already racing at maximum speed, south to a point on the continent.

<The Leerans don't need the continent. They are quite happy in their underwater cities,> Galuit said. <But there's been some kind of problem with setting off the bombs. Our forces were overrun much too quickly. With the *Ascalin*'s forces we should have held out longer. The main switch was never armed. We've been beaming the destruct signal for hours. Nothing. And the Yeerks will soon discover our trap. It's now or never.>

I hesitated. Should I tell Galuit why our forces were so easily overrun? I took a deep breath. <Sir, the *Ascalin* was never in the fight.>

Galuit swiveled both stalk eyes toward me. <What?>

<Captain Samilin was . . . a traitor,> I said. <He set the ship toward a landing behind Yeerk lines. He was killed. Once it was clear the *Ascalin* could not escape, Tactical Officer Harelin made the decision to fire all weapons while on

the ground. No one survived. Except for us and two of our friends who have disappeared.>

I could see Galuit slump. He seemed suddenly older. More frail.

"Why us?" Marco asked. "Why do you need *us* to go in and arm this switch?"

<We have few Andalites here on the planet now. And none who possess the wide array of morphs you have,> Galuit explained. <All Andalite warriors are morph-capable. But few *acquire* morphs or use them. That is mostly done by our people in intelligence. Spies. But you four may be able to penetrate the Yeerk forces.>

Suddenly he looked confused. His eyes went left, then right. <I was sure it was four. Where is the other human?>

A cold lance of fear struck my hearts. Prince Jake was still there. Cassie, too. But Marco . . .

"Marco!" Prince Jake cried.

"Marco! Marco!"

<We are disappearing one by one!> I said.

Galuit yelled a thought-speak summons that was heard clear through the submarine. <Science officer, report to me, right now!>

"This is insane!" Cassie said, her eyes blazing. "What is happening? One by one we're disappearing."

Cold fear wormed through my insides. I felt

sorry for Marco and the others. Very sorry. But now I was more afraid than anything. It didn't take too much imagination to figure out that the rest of us would be disappearing eventually.

It's one thing to face an enemy. It's very different to wait, powerless, for some unseen force to simply . . . delete you.

The sub raced on through the bright Leeran sea. But there was no time to enjoy the view. Prince Jake, Cassie, and I were surrounded by Andalites. We were cross-examined by the sub's science officer. In between questions from him we were bombarded by questions from Galuit and a counterintelligence officer.

It was nerve-racking. But at least it kept my mind off the awful suspense of waiting . . . waiting . . . waiting for another one of us to disappear.

<How long were you in Zero-space?>

<Are you sure Captain Samilin knew the ship was heading for Yeerk lines?>

<What was the mass of the creature you morphed on Earth before being dragged into Zero-space?>

<Did Captain Samilin seem embittered, stressed?>

At last, after an hour, Galuit put an end to it. <Enough! Samilin was a traitor. We have to ac-

cept that.> He turned to the science officer. <And you've asked the same questions fifty times. Give me a hypothesis.>

<Sir, I don't have enough —> the science officer started to say.

<Just give me your best guess!> Galuit demanded.

<I . . . I think these humans and this *aristh* are still caught in a residual flux field. It is pulling them back toward Zero-space. It may even be snapping them all the way back to Earth. But my best guess is that what's happening is a sort of elastic effect. They were stretched through Zero-space and back into normal space, but a small amount of their mass is still back on Earth. It may be acting like an anchor.>

"We're on some big Zero-space rubber band?" Prince Jake asked. "It's been stretching all this time, and now it's starting to snap back?"

<Yes,> the science officer said, after I explained what a rubber band was.

"Maybe all the way back to Earth, in which case Rachel and Tobias and Marco are alive," Cassie said. "Or maybe just into Zero-space. In which case . . ."

<From the data you've given me, the effect appears to be accelerating,> the science officer said. <You will go, one by one, faster and faster now. Like your friends, you will each disappear.>

Galuit said, <Under these circumstances, I cannot ask you to carry out this mission.>

Prince Jake shrugged. "Under these circumstances, it doesn't look like we have anything to lose."

CHAPTER 25

We were briefed by one of Galuit's officers.

<The central arming unit is well hidden. It is in what the Leerans call a "bright hole." Here on Leera the volcanic past created a number of large, underground bubbles in the rock. Because the rock contains a great many phosphorescent minerals and bio-organisms, there is light in these holes, and thus, life.>

"What kind of life?" Cassie asked. Even now, she was interested in living things.

<Plant only, aside from insects and microscopic animals. This particular "bright hole" can only be reached two ways: Either someone on the surface must tunnel down through several feet of

rock. Or one must travel underwater, up a river, enter an underwater cave, pass through an absolutely lightless tunnel, and emerge at last in the "bright hole.">

Prince Jake took a deep breath. Cassie took a deep breath. I took a deep breath. We each looked at each other.

Galuit said, <That's not all. The river itself may be guarded by Leeran-Controllers. The lightless cave is inhabited by a species of snake that uses echolocation to strike at anything passing by. These snakes hang from the ceilings and walls. But once within the "bright hole" you are safe. Unless, of course, the Yeerks have already found it.>

"Is it too late for us to change our minds?" Prince Jake said.

Galuit looked alarmed.

<It is humor,> I said quickly. <Human humor often consists of pretending to wish something one does not really wish.>

"What makes you so sure I don't mean it?" Prince Jake muttered.

<More humor,> I explained to Galuit.

The submarine took us to the mouth of the river. It was as close as it could take us without becoming far too visible for safety.

"I know the oceans are saltwater here, just

like on Earth," Cassie said. "But how about the rivers?"

<The rivers are lower saline,> the briefing officer said.

Cassie shook her head. "Hammerheads are saltwater fish. I don't know how they'd deal with freshwater. I just don't know. But they're still probably the best morph for moving fast and winning fights."

<Good luck,> Galuit said. <The freedom of this planet rests on your tails. Or . . . or whatever humans have that would be the equivalent of tails.>

"Shoulders," Cassie said.

"As long as there's no pressure," Prince Jake said.

<That would be human humor?> Galuit asked.

"Plus a little human fear," Prince Jake said. But then he laughed.

Five minutes later, we were in the river, swimming against the current, our dorsal fins slicing upward into the air.

<This should be interesting,> Prince Jake said darkly.

<I smell Leerans,> I said. <Up ahead. I recognize the smell from before.>

<Yep,> Cassie agreed. <Good Leerans or bad? That's the question.>

We powered ahead. Through the slightly murky river water we saw them: two pebbly, yellow, tentacled amphibians.

Psychic amphibians.

As soon as we were within range of them, the Leerans knew what we were. They turned and swam away as if their lives depended on it.

<After them!> Prince Jake cried.

They were heading for the banks of the river. Trying to get up, out of the water, beyond our reach. They didn't have water jets, just their natural Leeran bodies.

We were faster, but the bank was close, closer! The water grew shallow. No more than seven feet. Five feet! The Leerans were kicking up mud, but my shark senses could feel the electrical field of the Leerans now.

Blind, scraping my belly in mud, I lunged.

My teeth bit down. I clamped and held on and struggled to pull the creature back out into the water.

But then, up through the ripply surface I saw a huge, looming Hork-Bajir. Two, no, four of them! They came stomping out into the water. I pulled back. I tried to turn as the Leeran kept fighting me.

Then I heard the Leeran's psychic cry to the Hork-Bajir. *Explosives! The whole continent is*

rigged to explode. There's a central switch. Bright hole! It's in a —

I bit down harder. The pain stopped the Leeran from saying more. A Hork-Bajir blade slashed down into the water. It sliced me, but not deep.

I let go of the Leeran, jerked my head right, bit down with all my might on the nearest Hork-Bajir's leg. I heard a howl of pain come burbling down through the water.

The Leeran was scrambling away. Still half-blind, I lunged.

The Hork-Bajir had backed off. And now I dragged the Leeran-Controller back out into deeper water.

<No!> the Yeerk in his head cried.

<Oh, yes,> I said. I swept behind him and bit off the lobe at the back of his head. Out came the Yeerk.

<Are you okay, brother Leeran?> I asked.

I am now. Thank you, my Andalite friend! Hurry. Hurry! The Yeerks know your mission now! Hurry!

I turned back upstream. Cassie and Jake fell in beside me. They had each had their own battles in the murky, shallow water.

<How long will it take the Yeerks to find this "bright hole"?> Prince Jake asked.

<Using the sensors aboard their orbiting

ships, they will have a map of every subsurface cavern on the continent within five minutes. How long to find the right "bright hole"? I don't know. We must hurry. The fate of this planet depends on us.>

CHAPTER 26

<There! Is that the underwater cave entrance?> Cassie cried.

<I think so. It's in the right area. But there could be dozens of caves.>

<No time to worry about it,> Prince Jake said.

We plunged into the mouth of the cave. The floor rose steadily and we swam on grimly, blind, scared, and in a desperate hurry.

Suddenly I felt my snout break the surface. Air!

<I think we're there,> Prince Jake said. <Demorph! Cassie, what do you think? Bat morphs?>

There was no answer.

<Cassie! Cassie!> Prince Jake cried.

<The rubber band effect. She's gone. Back to Earth. Or . . .>

<It's happening faster,> Prince Jake said. <Less time between people disappearing. Just two of us now. We could both be snapped back before we reach this switch.>

He sounded like I felt. Like he couldn't breathe. Like he couldn't stop his heart from pounding. It was too much!

<Demorph. Nothing to do now but hurry and try to get this job done!> Prince Jake said.

<Yes, Prince Jake,> I said.

<You know, Ax, there's just the two of us now. We could probably drop the whole "prince" thing.> He paused, then added, <You could just call me "The Jake formerly known as Prince.">

<Is that a bit of humor?>

<Yeah. A joke. Not much of one, but Marco isn't here, so I figure . . .>

At that point he made the transition to mostly human and lost his thought-speak ability. I emerged as Andalite, standing in a cold, absolutely black cave, with water still sloshing over my hooves.

"Bat," Prince Jake said. His mouth-sounds echoed slightly.

I focused on the bat. I felt myself shrinking,

although there was nothing to see for comparison. But I could almost feel an upward breeze as I dropped from my own height down to the stumpy, few inches of the bat.

<Just you and me now, Ax.>

<Yes.>

<If one of us is stopped, for any reason, the other one has to keep going. Clear?>

We fired echolocation bursts and saw the sketchy portrait of a cave that stretched on and on, far past our faintest ultrasonic echoes.

We took to wing. We flapped up on leather wings and raced at full, tearing speed.

<We have to remember the snakes,> I said.

<Ugh. Ughughugh,> Prince Jake said with a sort of shudder.

<Yes,> I agreed.

We flapped as if our lives depended on it. Through jutting rocks and stalactites, around sudden turns, up sudden chimneys, and down sudden wells. All of it reduced to colorless lines in our mind's eye. A sketch drawn with blasts of sound.

Around one hairpin turn and suddenly . . .

A blast of sounds! A cacophony of echolocating squeaks and trills.

<The snakes!> I cried.

Our own echolocation showed them as writhing

lines that hung from the low ceiling and reached out from the walls. There were thousands! Millions! All firing their own echolocations, yammering and confusing the echoes of our own blasts.

Suddenly, in all the ultrasonic noise, the pictures in my head became distorted. Wild, swerving, swooping lines. Writhing borders of objects that no longer seemed solid.

<What do we do?> Prince Jake asked.

<As Rachel would say if she were here: We go for it!>

It was a nightmare! Deadly snakes filled the air. Lost, confused, we powered on, flapping wings that became more and more shredded as more and more snakes found their target.

I was losing maneuverability. Losing speed. I had lost sight of Prince Jake altogether. I could no longer tell up from down. I was spinning, flapping madly, afraid and confused. Lost! Lost in a squirming madhouse of darkness.

And then, swoosh! I blew free of the snakes. The cave walls backed off. The ceiling was gone. And light! Blessed light was glowing all around me.

I was in the "bright hole."

I soared upward on tattered, shredded wings. Up into the stale air. Everywhere flowers and plants in absurd colors exploded from the walls of the hole.

<Prince Jake! Jake!> I called.

But there was no answer.

Quite suddenly, I was all alone.

CHAPTER 27

I landed on a clump of screamingly orange mold or lichens or . . . something. And began to demorph.

Within minutes I was standing alone, an Andalite in a bizarre underworld universe cut off from the world outside.

The "bright hole" was perhaps five hundred feet at its longest, half that wide. The roof was no more than a hundred feet over my head. It was very large for a hole in the ground. But it felt very small.

No rain had ever fallen here. No sun had ever shone here. The only light was from the greenish glow of the walls. A light that never grew brighter, never grew dim.

It was alive, but dead-feeling. A wonder of nature, but a creeping, spirit-crushing place.

In the center of the place was the only artificial object: a vertical cylinder, five feet tall, a foot in diameter. On the side was a control pad, showing glowing blue numbers. Right where Galuit had said it would be. Just as Andalite intelligence agents had placed it.

I looked cautiously around. But I saw no Hork-Bajir, no Taxxons, no Gedds. Just unnatural plants in an unnatural place.

I exhaled, trying to shed my tension. <Whoever decided to hide this thing here sure picked a good hiding place,> I said.

I began to trot toward the cylinder. But the ground was rough, rising, falling, overrun with mosses and molds and clumps of hideous flowers. There were no paths.

I ended up having to step carefully, only able to hurry when I was sure of a place to leap.

Ba-WHOOOOM!

An explosion rocked the room. The concussion, trapped in that hole, knocked me off my feet and left me temporarily deaf.

Brilliant light!

Falling rock and debris.

A hole had been blown into the top of the "bright hole." Leeran sunlight streamed down in a blinding shaft.

And down, down through the shaft of light, the Hork-Bajir dropped.

Their fall was slowed by small rockets on their feet and tails. The rockets burned red. Two, four, a dozen Hork-Bajir warriors falling in slow motion, unlimbering their Dracon beams. I could see them peering about as they fell, searching for the cylinder. And for me.

I ran. I didn't care if I broke a leg. I ran, I leaped, I fell and lurched back up.

It was a race between falling Hork-Bajir and me.

Tseeewww!

ZzzzaaaaPPPP!

The Dracon beam stabbed at me, missed, and boiled a bright blue cabbage into steam.

Just a few more feet!

Suddenly, my hands were pressed on the cold metal. The code! What was the code?

My fingers flew.

Tssseeewww! Tseeewww!

"*Het gafrash nur!*" a Hork-Bajir screamed.

Tsseeewww!

<Aaaahhh!> I felt a burn across my back, a glancing blow from a Dracon beam.

The code! The code! I entered it. Was I right? Had I remembered?

Then . . .

<System armed.> The cool, thought-speak

voice of the computer. <Warning. This system is armed.>

I collapsed, leaning back against the cylinder. Galuit had said once they got confirmation that we had armed the system, they'd wait half an hour to give us time to escape.

Half an hour would be too long. The Yeerks would be able to disarm it by then.

A huge Hork-Bajir hit the ground right in front of me.

I punched the built-in communicator on the cylinder. <This is *Aristh* Aximili,> I said. <Do it now. Do it *now*! Blow the Yeerks off this planet!>

"*Filshig* Andalite!" the Yeerk inside the Hork-Bajir screamed.

I was calm. Shockingly calm.

<Detonation in ten seconds,> the computer warned.

"Disarm that weapon!" the Hork-Bajir commander yelled, switching to *Galard*, the interstellar language.

<Seven . . .>

<I don't think so, Yeerk. This time you lose. This time, you die.>

<Five . . .>

The Hork-Bajir raised his Dracon beam in rage. "You'll die first, Andalite scum!"

<Three . . .>

He squeezed the trigger.

The Dracon beam fired. Point-blank range. Five feet from my face.

<One . . .>

I literally saw the Dracon beam stop. The beam stopped in midair as time froze. I heard a "pop!"

And suddenly, I was no longer there.

CHAPTER 28

I felt the warm, human skin beneath my six legs.

<What?> I yelped.

<What the . . . ?> Rachel yelled.

<Whoa! Whoa, I am serious: Whoa!> Marco cried. <This is way too strange.>

I was back. On Earth. In mosquito morph.

We were all back. All back! And all at the same exact moment.

We were in the hospital room, surrounded by human-Controllers who were busy firing human guns out the window at the bushes below. Still trying to kill the Andalite.

Me.

But that was not the biggest problem I had. Because right then, as I sat on vibrating human flesh, surrounded by giant hairs, a huge, sky-filling object came hurtling down toward me.

<No way!> Rachel yelled. <Ax, move out!>

I fired my wings.

The object, five fingers each as big around as a large tree, came slapping down at me.

"Ow!" said Hewlett Aldershot the Third, as he slapped the spot where I'd been busily biting him.

"Ow!" he said again.

"The human! He's awake!" one of the human-Controllers said.

"He's not supposed to wake up yet!" another moaned. "He's in a coma!"

"What do we do?"

"The Visser will kill us!"

"The police are coming. We can't be taken!"

"Run! Run!"

"What do we do with this Aldershot human?"

"We have no orders,"

"Run!" someone yelled again. And this time, the rest agreed.

There came a loud vibrating thunder as the human-Controllers all raced from the room in a panic.

Moments later, a frightened nurse came in.

"Mr. Aldershot! You're . . . you're conscious."

"Of course I'm conscious," he said. "Nurse, are you aware that this room is full of mosquitoes?"

CHAPTER 29

"So wait a minute here," Rachel said. "We get zapped back here through Zero-space, one by one, at different times. But when we get back here, we all arrive at the same moment? And no time has passed?"

I nodded my human head. We were at the mall. At the place where the excellent food places are. I was in human morph. Behaving perfectly like a human. "Exactly, Rachel. Eggs-ACT-lee. Zactly. We arrived back at the precise moment when we were snatched away. We were all yanked away at the same moment, so naturally we all arrived back at the same moment. Yanked. Yanked is a strange word. Yank. Yank-kut."

"Yeah," Marco said. "*That's* what's strange:

the word 'yanked.' Us turning into mosquitoes to suck some guy's blood so we could morph into him and instead ending up in the middle of some war to control psychic yellow frogs, and oh, by the way, blowing up a small continent full of Yeerks, saving an entire species, then getting back here to find out Coma-man woke up from a mosquito bite delivered by a morphed alien-slash-deer-slash-scorpion-slash-four-eyed centaur, *that's* all totally normal. That's just an average day. Dear Diary: another boring average day, till someone said 'yanked.'"

I recognized his tone. Sarcasm. It is a form of humor. So I laughed using mouth-sounds.

"Hah. Hah-hah. Hah. Hah." I considered, then added, "Hah."

Prince Jake, Cassie, Marco, Rachel, and Tobias, in his own human morph, all stared at me.

"What was that?" Rachel demanded.

"I laughed."

"Don't . . . don't do that, Ax," Prince Jake said. "It's disturbing somehow."

"Yes, Prince Jake."

"Don't call me prince."

"I will call you 'The Jake formerly known as Prince.'"

Marco made a horrified face. "Oh, no. Now he's making jokes. Bad, bad jokes."

"Actually, that was my joke," Prince Jake said

stiffly. "Oh, fine. I get it. You can't laugh at *my* jokes. Okay. Great. I don't even care."

I was an Andalite, all alone, far, far from home. Far from my own people. Except that sometimes your own people are not just the ones who look like you. Sometimes the people who are your own can be very different from you.

"Can we eat cinnamon buns now?" I asked hopefully. "Bun-zuh?"

Don't miss

ANIMORPHS

<MEGAMORPHS #2>

#2 In the Time of Dinosaurs

“What should we do, Prince Jake?” Ax wondered.

“Have I mentioned don't call me prince?” Jake said automatically.

“Yes, Prince Jake, you have.”

Jake looked around. “I guess we go that way,” he said, pointing to the forest. “But not along *that* path. Whatever crushed those trees and made these tracks, we don't want to run into it. But obviously, wherever we are — some island somewhere, Africa, South America — wherever we are, there have to be people, right? Just not here on the beach. So let's go find them.”

I found myself looking back at the sea, at the surf that lapped almost peacefully on the coarse dark sand. Was she still alive somehow? Jake was right: If anyone could get swallowed by a whale — or whatever that thing had been — and survive, it was Rachel.

"I caught a glimpse of a clearing way back in the trees," I said. "Could be a village there."

Jake led the way into the trees. The sun was shut out by the tall, spreading branches. There were vines hanging down and crawling up the trunks of trees. And huge ferns so big you could hide in them.

We struck a stream, maybe fifteen feet across. Both banks of the river were lined by magnolias, dogwoods, and massive fig trees.

"This is not anywhere near being home," I said. "This is more like tropical vegetation."

"It's humid enough, that's for sure," Marco complained.

"I wonder if the water's okay to drink?" Jake asked. Then, with a shrug, he dropped to his knees and dipped his hand in. He brought the water to his mouth and sipped.

"I guess we can always get a bunch of shots for whatever disease is in the water," I said. I dropped beside him and tasted the water. The humidity hadn't seemed so bad down by the ocean. But now it was dehydrating me. I was massively thirsty.

"It's probably okay," I said. "Usually running water —"

FWOOOSH!

A huge head exploded from the water.

SNAP!

A jaw six feet long slammed shut with a sound like steel on steel. The jaw snapped shut so close to my face that it grazed my nose.

I leaped back. Fell on my butt. Spun, jumped up, and bolted.

"That was one big honkin' alligator!" Marco yelled as he ran beside me.

We stopped beneath a huge tree. Four of us, all panting.

"That wasn't right," I gasped.

"Yeah, no kidding," Marco said.

"No, I mean it was too big. The jaw was too long and thin."

"I am really not liking this," Jake muttered. "What were those things in the ocean? What made that footprint? Where on Earth are we that has crocodiles that size? I mean, we've seen crocodiles. That was one way, *way* big gator."

"Prince Jake, I am going to demorph," Ax said.

"Have you been in morph too long?" Jake asked with a frown.

"No. But I am frightened," Ax replied. "I don't want to have to fight in this weak human body."

"Yeah, go ahead," Jake said. "Cassie, I don't mean to hit you with this, but you know more about animals than any of us. Where the — where on Earth are we?"

"I don't know," I admitted. "Giant crocodiles, huge, aggressive whales or whatever, like nothing I've ever even heard of, and something big enough to leave a footprint you could turn into a wading pool. I just don't know."

"Okay, fine," he said, obviously frustrated. "Let's try it another way. Ax, you know more about physics and so on than any of us —"

"More than *any* human," Ax said. He was demorphing but was still mostly human.

"Whatever. Just tell me how an explosion could have blown us all the way to, I don't know, Madagascar or wherever, without killing us."

"Madagascar?" Marco asked.

"It couldn't," Ax said simply.

"Great. Great. That clears everything up just fine. This is nuts." He sighed. He looked at me and shrugged.

"I don't know," I said. "Maybe when we find some people they can tell us where we are."

We walked on, heading toward the clearing. The forest had become a frightening place to us. Everything was wrong. Out of place somehow, in some way I couldn't quite explain. How had the storm and rain suddenly become humid sunlight? How had we gone into the water off a beach fronted by a boardwalk and come out at a beach fronted by forest?

"Maybe it's all a dream," Marco said, as if

he'd been reading my thoughts. "In which case, I'd like to dream about a nice, ice-cold Coke." He held out his hand, curved around an imaginary bottle. "Hmm. So much for the dream theory."

We were almost to the clearing now. I could see bright, buttery sunlight through the trees. But massive ferns blocked my view of the clearing itself.

"Let's get out from under these trees," I said. "We'll think better in the open. And maybe there will be some people."

"Too bad they'll speak Madagascarese," Marco said.

"Shhh!" I froze.

"What?"

"Shhhh! Listen!" A grunting, snuffling sound to our left. Then the sound of greenery being rustled. Then more snuffling. The sound of . . . eating? "Something munching leaves," I said.

"There's been way too much munching already," Marco muttered.

"No, it's okay," I said. "If it eats plants, it won't eat *us*. Could be a cow. If it's a cow, maybe it belongs to someone."

"And if it doesn't belong to anyone, maybe we can eat *it*. I'm starving."

We threaded our way cautiously toward the sound. The closer we got, the more confident I was. Yes, something was grazing. But did cows eat leaves? No. Deer, maybe?

I pushed aside a fern frond. And there it was.

It was perhaps twenty feet long from head to tail. It stood on four elephantlike legs. It had a long neck that made up a third of its length and was balanced by the long tail of equal length. Along its back were bumpy, bony things, like armor plating that only covered that one area.

For about two minutes I don't think one of us drew a breath. We just stared.

"I think it's a baby," I said.

"A baby?" Marco said. "Cassie, it's a dinosaur."

Suddenly.

Crash! Crash! CRASH! CRASH!

From behind us!

"HuuuuRROOOOAAARR!"

The ground shook from the impact of its huge, taloned feet. The blast of its roar shivered the leaves and buckled my knees.

I spun around just in time to see it leap.

It jumped over us like we weren't even there. Jumped over us with its awful, hawklike talons. It landed with one huge foot on the ground and one holding the side of the "little" dinosaur.

Down came the head. That huge, square, familiar head.

The Tyrannosaurus opened its massive jaws

and closed them at the base of the baby dinosaur's neck.

I didn't know what was happening. My mind was gone. Gone in out-of-control terror.

We ran.

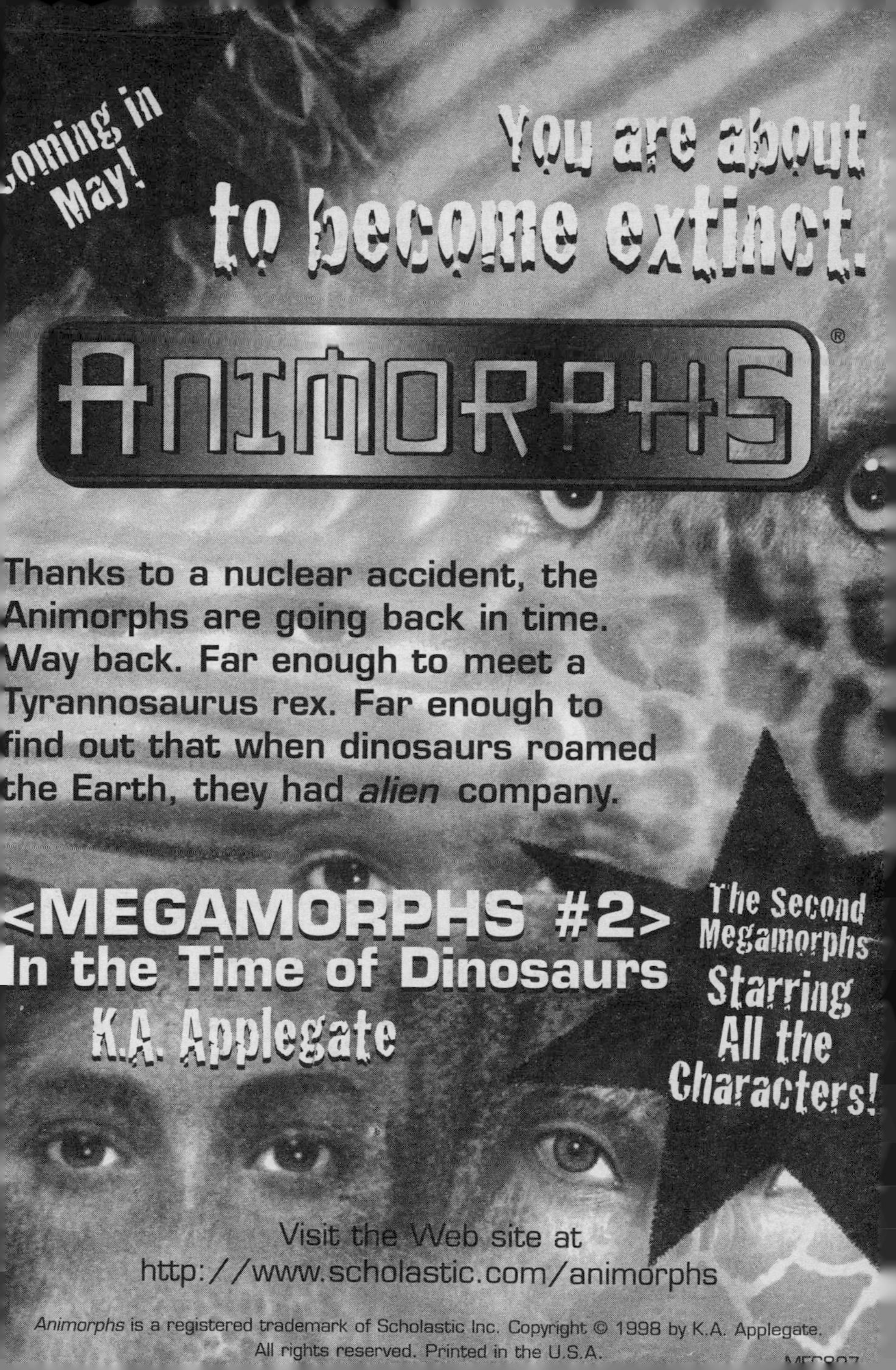
Coming in May!
You are about to become extinct.
ANIMORPHS®
Thanks to a nuclear accident, the Animorphs are going back in time. Way back. Far enough to meet a Tyrannosaurus rex. Far enough to find out that when dinosaurs roamed the Earth, they had *alien* company.
<MEGAMORPHS #2>
In the Time of Dinosaurs
K.A. Applegate
The Second Megamorphs
Starring All the Characters!
Visit the Web site at
http://www.scholastic.com/animorphs
Animorphs is a registered trademark of Scholastic Inc. Copyright © 1998 by K.A. Applegate.
All rights reserved. Printed in the U.S.A.